*For Sophie, who all my stories
have been for.*

One

Lily Hargan was not happy. Edge, her new home town, was tiny and scruffy. One of those blink-and-you'll-miss-it seaside towns glimpsed from a car as you zoomed off somewhere more exciting. An in-between sort of place, all rugged cliff edges and sun-bleached shutters and lopsided pavements.

Lily was also tiny and scruffy, and you might have thought this similarity would inspire a little fondness for the town. Kindred spirits and all. You would be wrong.

Lily missed the city. She missed the buildings stretching to the sky, the noise, the rush of people, the thousands of stories piled in on top of each other. She liked to sit in the park, writing elaborate backstories for the people scurrying past. The woman in the enormous sunglasses was a famous actor in disguise. The one wheeling the old suitcase was on the run from her cruel family. The lady in the fancy coat? The greatest jewel thief in the world.

Here, the game was ruined. Everyone in Edge

knew everyone and that was that. They all had solid, mundane lives. What was anyone supposed to do with that?

Lily had felt a brief glimmer of hope on discovering that Edge had a pirate museum, and had packed her binoculars and a peanut butter sandwich and set off with the intention of finding some buried treasure, or at the very least some grisly pirate stories.

No luck. The museum was just a load of tatty old books filled with unreadable curly handwriting, pieces of smashed-up wood that might have once been pieces of boats, and photographs of the town that confirmed Lily's suspicion that it hadn't changed a bit in about a hundred million years. She couldn't believe they had managed to make *pirates* boring.

With nothing else to do, Lily had taken to sloping around her new house looking melancholy. Her mum either failed to notice or chose not to – she was relentlessly cheerful, bringing home pocketfuls of seashells and banging on endlessly about the wonders of fresh air. As far as Lily could see, there was plenty of air in the city. And it didn't smell like fish.

In the days leading up to the start of school, Lily had consoled herself that at least there was a hint of glamour in being the new girl – she was the mysterious stranger, the big-city girl, a swan in a flock of humdrum seagulls. But as the first day approached, her confidence wavered and cracked. Really, there was nothing fun about being the new girl.

The well-meaning smiles of her classmates sent irritation prickling across her skin. They felt sorry for her – she knew it. They pitied her for having no friends. She could just imagine their questions and polite, practised responses. *Oh, you're from the city? What do you think of Edge?* She'd rather die. Which was how she ended up eating her lunch in her English teacher's classroom.

Lily liked Ms Hanan. She laughed a lot, and with her bright lipstick and pretty patterned hijabs she seemed to be the most glamorous person that Edge had to offer. Not that there was really much competition.

Books were scattered around the classroom and

Ms Hanan encouraged Lily to dive in.

"It's one of my favourites."

Lily looked up. "What?"

Ms Hanan gestured to the book in Lily's hand. "*Charlotte's Web*. It's one of my favourites."

"Oh. Yeah, me too."

This particular copy was Lily's own. It was well worn and Ms Hanan's mouth twitched approvingly as she took in the battered cover and lovingly dog-eared pages. Lily had always surrounded herself with books. They were more reliable than people. A book would never break a promise to you. A book would never ask how you were just so it could talk about itself. A book would never have a super-annoying laugh. Books were always there, ready to sweep you up and hold you tight whenever you needed them. They were the perfect company.

She suddenly realised she'd been reading the same sentence over and over for about five minutes.

"I always saw a little of myself in the farmer's daughter," said Ms Hanan. "When I was a kid I was a sucker for a lost cause. Always coming home with jars of caterpillars and buckets of crabs and crying inconsolably when my dad told me we couldn't keep them."

Lily wrinkled her nose. She had always thought the farmer's daughter was a bit of a drip.

"I think I'm more of a Charlotte the spider."

Ms Hanan nodded. "That's a good thing to be. Intelligent. Loyal."

"Weird?"

"We all need a bit of weird in our lives, Lily. Weird is good."

Lily shrugged.

"She's independent too. Like you. But you know, her adventures begin when she's brave enough to make a friend."

Lily snapped the book shut. "Are we still talking about *Charlotte's Web*?"

Ms Hanan laughed. "I'm just making an observation. She might have spent her whole life in that barn corner if she hadn't worked up the courage and said hello to someone."

"She says 'salutations'."

"That's because she's a show-off."

"No point being smart if you're not going to show it off."

Ms Hanan shook her head. "You were right. You *are* a Charlotte. And that being the case, I'm going to set you some homework. I want you to do exactly what Charlotte does. I want you to make a friend. Well, nothing quite as hard as that. I want you to pick someone in the school and say hello to them before class on Monday."

Lily's head jerked up. "You can't set that as homework."

Ms Hanan's eyes were sparkling. She looked thoroughly pleased with herself. "Watch me."

"But, miss!"

"No. No buts. I expect you to arrive in my class on Monday morning with your homework completed."

"But everyone here is so..." Lily let the sentence trail off under Ms Hanan's arching eyebrow.

"I'm not asking you to get married. Just say hello. I don't care if you yell it and then run away. Although people might find that a little strange."

"People already think I'm strange."

"They do not. Now, go and choose someone. They might surprise you."

Lily highly doubted it.

Two

Just like every other road in Edge, the one that Lily was on came out by the sea. The water lay dull and flat among the jagged rocks, waves sucking greedily at the shore. When her mum had told her they were moving to the seaside, she had at least hoped for pristine white sands like you saw on TV.

Edge's beaches weren't like that at all. The sand was dark and generously peppered with pebbles and seashells. Seaweed streaked its surface and little pools thrived in the craggy rocks, teeming with life. Lily refused to be interested in any of it, despite her mum's enthusiasm. There were a few families dotted on the sand now, building castles, writing their names with enormous sticks. She sighed heavily and turned away to head home.

The street curved away in front of her. She hadn't been down this way before but she guessed it must be close enough to where she had been aiming. The whole town seemed like it was about a hundred steps across, so anywhere was close enough really.

She turned left down the next alley and frowned. It looked exactly the same as the last one.

The tall whitewashed houses were strung out in front of her like sheets of paper, with colourful doors and neat window boxes. Lily tore a flower out of one and then suddenly felt guilty. She tucked it back in. At the end of the road, she stopped dead. Another identical street. She was definitely lost. She started to wonder if she was having a nightmare. An endless road of Edge houses, twisting around her for all eternity.

She tried to retrace her steps to work out which direction the main road was in, but the curving streets threw her. The whisper of the sea was ever present. She took out her phone and started to type in her mum's name, then stopped and stuffed it back into her pocket. She was twelve years old. She couldn't phone her mum and tell her she'd got lost like a little kid. Besides, she didn't even know how to describe where she was. *Oh yeah, I'm on that street that looks like all the other streets. Hope you find me before I starve to death!* She would just have to find her way home.

She wasn't really sure what made her notice the door. It sat between two identical white houses, so narrow it was almost invisible. It was painted dark glossy green and was slightly ajar. Lily sidled up to it. The gap between the door and its frame was furred with cobwebs. She tried to peer through, but all she could see was gloom. She suddenly couldn't shake the feeling that there was something waiting for her behind the door.

She put her palm flat on the wood and gave it a tentative push. It swung open, sending tiny puffs of dust spinning into the air. This was a door that hadn't been touched in a long time.

To Lily's surprise, it opened to reveal a thin spiral staircase. A tiny golden arrow was nailed to the wall, pointing upwards. Lily glanced behind her. There was no one around. She should try to get home really. She was already running late. On the other hand, this was the only interesting thing she'd found since moving to Edge.

She slid round the door and started to climb the

stairs. At the top was another wooden door, also slightly ajar. There was a small brass sign fixed to it, bearing the word "Museum". She wiped the dirt from a second, smaller sign underneath and bent to read the curling copperplate writing. *The Museum of Emily*.

Lily stood blinking at the sign for a moment. Whatever she had been expecting, this wasn't it. She pushed open the door and entered the museum. There was a low wooden desk in front of her, but no one behind it. Everything was coated in a thick layer of dust and she fought to hold back a sneeze. As she approached, she saw a shiny bell on the desk, like in old-fashioned hotels, and couldn't stop a delighted smile spreading over her face. Lily pressed the bell, taking great pleasure in its rich *ding*.

"Service, please," she said loudly.

The sound of the bell echoed briefly around the space and then died away. No one came. Lily cleared her throat gently.

"Hello?" she called. "I'd like to visit the museum."

She started to feel silly, and turned to go back down

the stairs, but stopped when she reached the door. She traced the letters of the sign with her fingertips. Emily had planted herself firmly in Lily's mind, like an itch. With a sigh, Lily returned to the desk.

"Hello-o?" she shouted one more time, just to be sure.

Then, confident that there was no one coming, she slipped round the back of the desk and started snooping. Being behind the desk felt illicit and thrilling. The top two drawers were annoyingly empty, the bottom two intriguingly locked. She yanked on them but the locks were sturdy and didn't give.

Remembering a book she had read where someone could pick any lock with a hairpin, she fished around in her unruly curls. Result! She tugged the clip from her hair, blowing the falling strands out of her eyes. She crouched in front of the lock and inserted the hairpin into it. She wiggled it around, ear pressed to the drawer, listening for a click. Nothing. Shaking her head, she tried to pull the pin back out again. It was stuck. Of course it was. She pulled harder and the metal snapped, pinging into the lock. She cursed as loudly as she dared and gave the drawer a hopeful wiggle. No luck.

There was a tiny window behind the desk, spilling sunlight into the room. The dust filling the air carved the light into a thick, solid slice, constantly shifting and changing. It made Lily's head spin a little. She stood on her tiptoes and looked through. A laugh forced its way out and she rolled her eyes. She could see the main road. She must have been a street or two away the whole time. She returned to the front of the desk and read the small white placard standing to one side.

Welcome to the Museum of Emily.
Please follow the arrows.

An arrow pointed to a dark entryway on the left. Lily looked at her phone. She was pretty late. But given that she was already pretty late, there was no sense in rushing off now. Besides, she was only a few minutes from home, now that she knew where she was. Might as well have a look around.

The room that Lily entered was oddly shaped, long and narrow. Glancing back at the spiral staircase, she realised that it must run parallel to the alleyway outside. This was what lay behind the facade of one of the white houses. She stood still, letting her eyes adjust to the gloom, and shapes began to come into focus around her. Soft light leaked from an overhead bulb, casting long, wild shadows against the walls.

One wall was blank, covered in dark wood panelling. Stretching the length of the opposite wall was an exhibition case. In the case Lily could see an assortment of glass boxes, black frames and small drawers, each labelled with a neat white rectangle. At the very end of the room was another doorway, upon which there was a gold arrow, pointing downwards.

The air felt heavy and musty, and no sounds from the outside world seeped in, not even the ever-present sea. Which was why the sudden vibrating of her phone made Lily jump about a metre in the air. She pulled it out, her heart hammering hard against her ribs. Her mum. She winced, bracing herself.

"Hello?"

"Lily Hargan, where on *earth* are you?"

"I'm really sorry, Mum. I meant to call."

"I've been worried sick about you."

"I know, I'm sorry. I meant to phone but I forgot. I'm ... just hanging out with a friend."

"A friend?" Her mum's voice filled with undisguised happiness. "I thought you didn't like anyone in Edge?"

"Er, yeah, she's a new friend."

"Who is she?"

"Er, her name is Emily. She's ... in my class at school."

"Well, that's lovely, sweetheart. I'm glad you're settling in."

Lily rubbed her forehead. "Yeah, it's great."

"I'm just starting on dinner, so..."

"Yeah, I'll leave now. Be home soon."

"We've got plenty here, so you're welcome to invite Emily along."

"No!" yelled Lily. She cleared her throat and forced her voice back down to a reasonable level. "No, she can't today. She's having dinner with her family."

"Oh. Next time then. She's always welcome. I'd like to meet her."

"Sure. See you soon."

"See you soon, love."

Lily hung up and gritted her teeth. There was no way her mum was going to forget about that. Where was she going to find a fake Emily in this dump of a town?

She approached the exhibition case and peered inside. The first exhibit was a small piece of paper inside a photo frame, yellowed with age and spattered with something dark and sticky-looking. Lily brushed the grime from the glass with her sleeve. The creases in the paper were deep and slightly furry, as though it had been folded and unfolded many times. It was covered in pretty, looping handwriting. Lily stooped to read the label.

Mum's apple pie recipe. As made on Emily's birthday.

Three

The house was filled with the smell of apples stewing. Normally that was the best thing about apple pie – even better than the first slice. The warm, sharp smell as the sugar melted into caramel, as the apples fell apart. But now it hooked Emily hard under the ribs.

It had been four days. Four days since someone had spotted her mum's little boat bobbing empty in the cove. Four days since the police had told them that anyone who went into that stormy water wasn't coming back out. And Emily hadn't believed it. She'd been so sure. They'd never seen her mum swim, didn't understand that she belonged to the sea, that the sea would never hurt her. But now it was Emily's birthday and her mum hadn't returned.

"You've got too much water," said Caitlyn. "That's why it's sticking."

Caitlyn was Emily's older sister.

"I'm following Mum's recipe," said Emily. "That's how much water she says to put in."

"That's not how baking works," said Caitlyn, sprinkling flour on to the sodden dough on the counter. "It's like magic. You have to feel it."

She put her hands on top of Emily's, showing her how to knead in the flour. The dough started to come together and stopped sticking to the surface. Emily fetched the rolling pin, mouth set in a grim, determined line. Caitlyn put a hand on top of her head.

"Hang on." She dipped her finger and thumb into the bag of flour and smeared a little on Emily's nose. She did the same with her own. "There, perfect. Now we can roll."

Emily's mouth twitched, just a little.

"Tell me a story. Tell me about Grandpa and the pirate."

"I've told you that one a million times," said Caitlyn, but she wasn't really protesting. She loved telling the story as much as Emily loved hearing it. An old family folk tale, moulded and remoulded by each generation.

"Well, it was hundreds of years ago, back when our family still owned the lighthouse, and Great-

Great-Grandpa John kept the light burning, just like his father had, and his father before him." Caitlyn paused to stir the apples, filling the kitchen with sweet-smelling steam as she lifted the lid of the pot. "That night, there was a great storm. Lightning tearing the sky apart, winds howling, rain beating against the lighthouse so hard that Grandpa John thought the glass might crack. But it held and he kept the flame lit, even though he knew no one would be mad enough to sail in that weather."

"Well, *almost* no one," said Emily.

Caitlyn nodded seriously. "That's right. Because as the light swung round on to the frothing sea, he saw the impossible."

"A boat!"

"The remains of a boat. And a man, half drowned, clutching on to the wreckage." Caitlyn's voice hitched slightly on the words. She swallowed. Emily looked up at her but her face remained calm and impassive. "Now, Grandpa John had a choice to make. He knew that he'd be risking his life if he went to help the man. But he also knew that it was his duty. So he readied his boat and rowed out into the storm."

Emily draped her pastry over the pie dish, pushing it down into the corners.

"The boat almost capsized more than once, and Grandpa John inhaled litres and litres of seawater."

"His chest was never the same again."

"Never the same again. But he was a master sailor. He kept his little boat steady and hauled the man to safety. He was near death when Grandpa John reached him, but he was brought in and sat by the fire, and little by little he started to recover. And it was then that he told Grandpa John his secret."

Caitlyn paused dramatically, pouring the stewed apples into Emily's pie crust. She leaned in close and, despite having heard the story a hundred times, Emily's heart quickened.

"The stranger was a pirate," whispered Caitlyn. "He had spent many years sailing to all corners of the world, boarding ships and stealing treasure where he could. But his close brush with death, and Grandpa John's brave actions, had taught him a lesson. He was going to change his ways. And to thank Grandpa

John, the pirate gave him a gift."

Caitlyn trimmed the edges of Emily's pastry lid with a sharp knife.

"A diamond," she said. "As big as a man's fist. He had stolen it from a queen, who had stolen it from someone else. It was worth millions. And now it belonged to Grandpa John."

Emily started to carve leaf shapes in the remaining scraps of pastry. "But..."

"But there was a problem. Great-Great-Grandpa John's eldest son was no good."

"He was a scoundrel!"

"A rascal!"

"The baddest of bad apples!"

"That's right. So Grandpa John hid the diamond somewhere very secret, away from his greedy, no-good son. And there it waits to this day, for someone sharp of brain and pure of heart to find it."

Emily sighed, pressing her pastry leaves on to the top of her pie. "I wish I had a diamond as big as a man's fist."

"Me too."

"Except wishes don't come true."

A tear slid from the end of her nose, dropping on to the floury counter. Caitlyn drew her close, burying her nose in Emily's hair. Then she pulled back, brushing her sister's tears away with her fingertips.

"We're going to be OK. There are other kinds of treasure."

Four

Monday morning arrived and Lily found herself in a panic about the non-completion of Ms Hanan's "homework". The museum had distracted her, occupying her thoughts throughout the weekend, but now the sight of school made it unavoidable.

She edged her way into the playground, trying to make eye contact with someone and then immediately dropping her gaze when she succeeded. Coward. She took herself off to one side for a stern talking-to. It was one word. Five seconds of her life. It didn't mean she had to be friends with the person. She could just say it, listen to whatever their boring response was and then go and tell Ms Hanan that she had tried but that she had been right to avoid her classmates all along. She steeled herself and went back into the playground.

Why did adults always feel as though they had to be helpful? They almost always made everything worse. She inwardly cursed Ms Hanan and looked around the playground. She had no idea how to just march up and insert herself into a conversation. As it turned out, she didn't have to.

"Hello."

Lily jerked her head up and found herself gazing into a pair of very large, very green eyes. A girl had appeared in front of her, smiling as though she'd known her all her life.

"H-hello," she said, blinking at the girl, half believing that she'd conjured her out of thin air.

The girl stuck out her hand. "I'm Sam. I think I live next door to you."

"Oh. Hi."

Lily had never shaken anyone's hand before. It felt pleasingly grown-up. Sam stuffed her hand back into the pocket of her tartan coat. She leaned against the wall and looked at Lily expectantly.

"What?"

"You not going to tell me your name?"

"Oh, yeah. Sorry. I'm Lily."

Lily nibbled at her thumbnail. She had been sure that the occupants of Edge would be just as small and dull as the town itself. But this girl looked interesting, patterned patches sewn into the knees of her trousers, hair swinging to her waist, a deep dimple in one corner of her mouth. She looked like... Lily shook the thought from her head before her stupid brain could finish it. The bell rang, signalling the start of the school day. Sam peeled herself reluctantly off the wall.

"Well, I'll see you later!"

Lily opened her mouth to reply but Sam was already gone, dark hair streaming behind her as she bounced down the corridor. She shrugged and started towards her first class.

At the end of the day, she found Sam sitting on the school wall, kicking her heels against the brick. When she saw Lily she waved frantically.

"Hello! I was waiting for you."

"Why?"

"Because you've been eating lunch on your own with a teacher and that sucks, so I thought we could walk home together. And because my friend Jay who normally walks with me is home with the flu, so if we don't walk together it's going to be you on your own with me walking on my own about two metres behind you. Which is creepy."

"OK."

"You don't talk very much, do you?"

"Sorry."

"That's OK, I talk far too much. We'll make a great pair. I can't imagine what it must be like to be the new girl. I've lived here my whole life. Is it scary moving to a new place? Do you like Edge?"

Lily scrunched up her nose. "I've never been anywhere less scary in my whole life. Things have to actually happen for something to be scary."

"Hey! This is my home town, you know."

"It's still boring."

"Give it a chance. It might surprise you."

"So people keep telling me."

"Do your parents like it?"

"It's just my mum and me. I think she likes it. She used to love living in the city and then she just ... didn't any more. So we came here."

"A house of girls! I'm so jealous. I've got two dads and two twin brothers and no girls at all. Even our *dog* is a boy. I always wanted a sister."

"Me too. I was always jealous of people with loads of siblings."

"You wouldn't think that if you met my brothers. They're the worst."

Lily kicked a pebble down the road. "I bet they're not."

"No, you're probably right. They're not the worst. They're just *boys*, you know? I kept begging my dads to get me a sister but that's not how it works *apparently*."

Lily didn't know what to say to that.

"Shall we be sisters then?" said Sam.

"What?"

"You and me. Shall we be sisters?"

Lily laughed. "You don't even know me."

"True. But I like you anyway. Even though you're kind of quiet and weird."

"Hey!"

Sam grinned and gave Lily a gentle push. "I'm only kidding. Sort of. You are a bit quiet and weird. But in a mysterious way. So how about it? Sisters!"

"I'll think about it."

They passed Sam's house, with its yellow gate and neat window boxes and honeysuckle climbing around the front door. Lily thought it was twee when she first moved in. Now it seemed kind of cute. Sam followed Lily straight past her house and into Lily's garden, still talking. Hearing the commotion, Lily's mum came out wearing ... was that an apron?

"Hello, hello. I thought that was you. And this must be Emily!"

Lily panicked. But Sam just smiled and shook her head.

"Oh no, not me. I'm Sam. I live next door."

"Oh! I met your parents earlier, Sam. I was expecting another boy."

Sam shrugged. "I get that a lot. I suspect they thought I was a boy until it was too late to return me."

Lily's mum laughed. "You're the photographer, is that right?"

"That's me."

"What do you take your photographs of?"

"Anything that catches my eye, really. Interesting things I see around town, mostly."

"Well, maybe you can get Lily interested in the town. Nothing I say seems to work."

Lily groaned.

"Are you in Lily and Emily's class too?"

"I am. Well, some of them."

Lily cleared her throat pointedly. Her mum turned slightly pink.

"Why don't I go and get you girls something to drink? Do you like lemonade, Sam?"

"I love lemonade, thank you so much, Ms Hargan."

Sam's smile stayed fixed as Lily's mum disappeared inside the house. The second the door closed behind her, Sam whipped her head round to face Lily. Lily wrapped her arms round herself.

"What?"

"Like I said, I've lived here all my life. And even if I hadn't, I'd *still* know the names of every girl in our school year. So who is Emily?"

Five

Lily's insistence that she didn't know who Emily was only made Sam more curious, and eventually, sensing that resisting was pointless, she told Sam that she'd show her.

That Saturday, Sam knocked on Lily's door. It was eight in the morning. Lily did not appreciate it one bit, but Sam smoothed things over by producing two enormous pain au chocolat from her coat pockets. Lily bit into hers, still warm from the oven, and chocolate oozed thickly into her mouth. It was delicious.

It was one of those autumn days where the sun barely drags itself above the horizon, skimming the rooftops of the town and stretching the shadows as thin and sharp as needles. Winding her way back through the streets with Sam, Lily wasn't sure she'd be able to find the door to the museum again. In fact, she started to wonder if she'd made it all up somehow. The whole thing was bizarre. It made more sense for it not to be there.

And yet, as the two rounded a corner, there it was. A green door in a white house, sitting inconspicuously between two other identical houses. Lily wondered how on earth she'd spotted it in the first place. In fact, Sam barged straight past at first, chattering away, and it took her a few steps to notice that Lily was no longer beside her. She looked from Lily to the door and back again.

"This is it? All that mystery just to show me someone's house?"

"It's not a house," said Lily, pushing the door open. "I don't really know what it is."

Sam's eyes lit up as the spiral staircase came into view. She turned a thrilled smile on Lily and squeezed her hand excitedly, before taking the stairs two at a time. There were a few moments of silence and then the sound of the bell floated down to Lily. She bit her lip to stop a spreading grin and followed Sam up. Sam was standing by the door, tracing the name of the museum with her fingertips.

"What is this place?"

"I have no idea. But come and see. You're not going

to believe it."

Lily passed Sam and pushed the door to the first room open. The hush of the museum and the quiet heaviness of the air stole the breath from her lungs again.

"Wow."

Sam's voice dropped to a whisper. She drew close to the wall, her nose stopping inches from the glass covering the apple pie recipe. Her eyes travelled the length of the room.

"I think it takes up two houses. At least," said Lily.

"It's amazing. What's in the next room?"

"I don't know. I haven't even looked at everything in this room yet. You haven't been here before then?"

"No way. I didn't even know this existed. How did you find it?"

"I don't really know. I just sort of ... did."

"What made you lie to your mum? About Emily?"

"I don't really know that either. It felt like the kind of thing a grown-up might not understand."

"I don't think *I* understand."

"Me neither."

"But I love it."

"Me too."

Lily leaned in close to an exhibit, trying to hide the smile on her face. They had a secret. Despite her best efforts, that felt good. There seemed to be no pattern to the exhibits, other than that they were all small, they were all unremarkable and they had all belonged to Emily. Well, more or less. Lily giggled at the label in front of her.

A lipstick, stolen from Caitlyn.

Another, a little further down read:

A pencil, loaned by Tony Ross.

Sam was bent over, examining a delicate pressed flower. It was paper-thin, the colour almost washed away by time and sunlight. Her fingerprints stood out against the dirt on the glass.

"I know these flowers," murmured Sam. "They grow in the cracks in the rocks. She must have been from around here."

"Yeah, thanks, genius. I'd guessed that."

Sam nudged Lily in the ribs affectionately, not taking her eyes off the flower. Her face split into a beaming grin. "It's a mystery. A real, full-blown mystery like in the movies."

"I know. What is all this stuff doing here?"

"I have no idea. Believe me, if anyone from Edge had done anything interesting enough to deserve a museum, I'd know about it. The only really interesting people we had were pirates, and they've got a museum of their own already."

"I don't think she was a pirate. That's not the feeling I'm getting. Everything here is so..."

"Ordinary," finished Sam. "But why would an ordinary girl have a museum?"

Lily made for the door on the other side of the room. "Come on, let's go and see what's downstairs."

The two girls followed the gold arrow at the far end of the room, painfully conscious of their footsteps echoing on the old staircase. It was even darker down here and as they approached the bottom of the stairs, they gasped in unison. Light spilled from an assortment of bulbs, as soft and yellow as candlelight. They were strung at different heights throughout the room, interspersed with hanging droplets of mirrored glass, which caught the light and spun it in the air. At the end of the room, just visible in the dancing light, was another arrow.

"I can't decide if it's wonderful or if it's creepy."

"Me neither."

Goosebumps rose on Lily's arms. She rubbed them away and walked towards the exhibits. Small everyday items, painstakingly labelled, just like on the floor above. She stopped in front of a copy of *James and the Giant Peach*, fuzzy with dust. Below, a label.

Emily's favourite.

Lily reached towards it. Sam slapped her fingers away.

"Were you raised in a barn? You can't touch things in a museum!"

"I'll be careful. I just want to look."

"Why?"

"A book can tell you a lot about a person."

Sam folded her arms but stepped out of Lily's way. Lily took the book in her hands and gently brushed the dust from the cover. It had clearly been well loved.

The cover was barely hanging on, and as she turned it in her hands Lily noticed that whoever had been reading it hadn't finished. The edge of a bookmark was just visible above the pages.

She gingerly edged it out, careful to keep a finger holding the place where it had been. Just in case Emily ever wanted to come back to it. Her face flashed with triumph. She waved the bookmark at Sam.

"Look! I told you!"

The bookmark was a small piece of card, with a gold star and the name "Emily McCrae" printed on it.

"Now we've got a full name to go on."

Sam took it from her, a slow smile dawning on her face.

"Even better. It's a clue. I know what this is. And I know exactly where we have to go."

"Where?"

Sam slipped the bookmark back into the book and returned it carefully to its place. She pulled an identical card from her own pocket. "To the place where all the mysteries live."

Six

The Edge library was bigger than seemed reasonable for such a small town, which was, in Lily's view, the perfect size for a library. Sam handed her card to Lily.

"That bookmark is her library card, see? Just like mine. Ms Bright gives you the gold sticker when you've borrowed a hundred books."

"So what do we do? Ask the librarian?"

"I don't think so. Ms Bright's only been here for a few years. There hasn't been anyone called McCrae in Edge the whole time I've lived here. Whoever Emily was, I don't think she's been into the library for a long time."

"So what then?"

"The library has all the town records. Births, deaths, marriages, adoptions, newspapers, everything. So—"

"So we use them to find out when the McCraes *did* live here."

They crossed under the enormous archway and Lily smiled. She was always amazed at how all libraries felt familiar. The stone walls, which had been gathering the sun's heat all morning, now released it with a sigh. The air was filled with the smell of paper. Slices of sunlight streamed through the high windows, illuminating the spaces between the bookshelves. There was a desk but no librarian, just a pile of books teetering haphazardly towards the ceiling.

"Ms Bright?" called Sam. "Ms Bright, it's Sam."

The voice that answered sounded like it was coming from miles away. "Hello, Sam! Sorry, I'm buried under a pile of books. Do you need me?"

"No, I think we're OK. I just want to have a look at the records again. Can I go ahead?"

"Sure you can. Just make sure you're gentle with them; they're very old."

"I will."

"If you're not sure whether to touch something, don't. Come and fetch me."

"I will."

"OK, sweetheart, go ahead."

"Thanks, Ms Bright," called Sam. "Are you OK? Do you need rescuing from the books?"

"No, they seem friendly. I'll shout if I get into any real trouble."

Sam chuckled. "She's a little eccentric," she whispered.

"All librarians are eccentric," came the voice, making the girls jump. "It's part of our charm."

"And she has the hearing of a bat, apparently. Come on, this is all fiction. The really good stuff is downstairs."

Lily followed Sam through the library and down a creaking set of wooden stairs. She was expecting piles of mouldering paper, covered in dust, made unreadable by age and wear; maybe a bare light bulb blinking menacingly overhead. When they arrived in the reference room, it was so entirely different that she gasped out loud.

Cardboard boxes were neatly labelled and stacked on dark wooden shelves, stretching from floor to ceiling. Shadows pooled conspiratorially between the shelves. The records themselves took up more than half of the room.

On the other side stood an enormous round table.

The surface was painted with a world map, sealed with glossy varnish. Lily put her hand on the surface. It was smooth and cool to the touch, tiny bubbles frozen under Lily's fingertips. Between every two chairs there was a heavy brass reading lamp. Off to one side, a trio of squashy green armchairs, lit by the same heavy lamps. She turned to face Sam, who was anxiously watching for her reaction. As their eyes met, she relaxed into a grin.

"It's amazing, isn't it? I think it's the coolest place in Edge. Well, maybe the second coolest now."

"It's brilliant."

"I come here all the time. I tell Ms Bright that I'm working on school projects but really I just like being nosy. I guess she probably knows that. She doesn't seem to mind, though."

Along the opposite wall to the shelves was a glass display case. Lily bent to look inside, sticking her hands in her back pockets to avoid the temptation to touch. On the far left was the town charter on curling yellow parchment. The rest of the town's history was displayed in an eclectic collection of artefacts, from smugglers' maps and records of pirate arrests, to political pin badges and protest signs.

"Cool, isn't it?" said Sam. "Ms Bright found all this stuff when she was sorting the town records. Donated loads to the museum – the town museum, that is, not the Emily museum – but kept a little of the historical stuff down here. Said things like this ought to be treasured."

Lily shook her head in wonder, backed away from the town's history and slung her coat on the back of a chair. "So where do we start?"

"Newspaper archives are over there. Official town records that way. I say we start with births and deaths; look for any McCraes we can find."

"Starting when?"

"There definitely haven't been any McCraes here since I've lived here, so it must be at least ten years ago."

"There's no way you could remember everything in the last ten years. I think we should start with five years ago and work our way back until we find them."

"Suit yourself. Do you want births or deaths?"

"I don't mind."

"You take deaths then. I'm not feeling particularly morbid today."

Sam hefted a couple of boxes from the shelves and set them between their two chairs.

"Put everything back exactly as it was. Ms Bright is pretty precious about all of this stuff. You're lucky it wasn't her book you grabbed in the Emily museum; she'd probably have chopped your fingers off."

With that comforting image, Lily pulled the first heavy book from her box. The spine crackled as she opened it and she winced, sneaking a glance at Sam, who was already absorbed in her task, pencil stuck behind her ear, tongue resting between her front teeth.

Lily used the hair band round her wrist to pull her hair out of her eyes. She arranged herself in a comfortable position and started to read.

At first, it was sort of fun. There was something exciting about holding history in your hands and she could make up stories to match the names and numbers on the page. After a while, though, the shine wore off. The registrar's handwriting was small and intricate, and squinting at it was giving Lily a headache. There was no pattern, no narrative, just hundreds of names on hundreds of pages and none of them were McCrae.

A glance at Sam told Lily that she was starting to feel the same way. Her eyebrows were pinched together, a deep crease of annoyance between them, and the top of her pencil was chewed to a pulp. She had a fleck of yellow paint in the corner of her mouth. Lily balled up a piece of paper and tossed it at her, bouncing it lightly off her chest. Sam's head jerked up, irritation written all over her face, and Lily recoiled for a second. The expression cleared almost immediately.

"Want to go for a walk or something?" said Lily.

"Sure. I've found nothing good."

"Me neither."

"Next time."

Warmth spread through Lily's chest. There was going to be a next time. They replaced the boxes where they had been and made their way back up the

48

stairs. By the time they arrived at the front desk, the librarian had emerged. Lily had expected an old lady but the woman at the desk looked about the same age as Lily's mum, pale-blonde hair falling in a tousled bob to her collarbone. She had a smudge of dust on her nose and grey eyes that crinkled in a smile.

"Oh, hello there. I was about to send down a search party. I thought you might have got lost."

Her eyes fell on Lily. "When you said 'we', I thought it must be you and Jay," she said to Sam.

"He's home with the flu. This is Lily. She's new."

"Well, when he's better, make sure to send him to me. I've got a fantastic book of sketches to show him. Hello, Lily. I'm Ms Bright."

"It's nice to meet you."

"What do you think of my library?"

"It's amazing. Really, really beautiful."

Ms Bright looked around, pleased. "I certainly think so. Would you like a library card?"

Lily left the library with her new card clutched in her hand, blowing on it to dry the ink and calculating how long it would take her to get a gold star like

Emily's. Her headache dissolved as the cold, damp air hit her and she found herself taking a deep breath, sucking the smell of the sea gratefully into her lungs.

Seven

Chaos reigned supreme at Sam's house. The second they opened the door, Lily was hit with a cacophony of sounds and smells. She instinctively took a step back but Sam took her by the hand and tugged her into the hallway.

"Dad! Papa! Come and meet my new friend Lily!"

A slim, birdlike man, all sharp edges and enormous square glasses, poked his head into the hall. He stuck out one hand, pushing his glasses up the bridge of his nose with the other.

"It's lovely to meet you, Lily. Will you be staying for—"

He was abruptly cut off as another man barrelled past. "So this is Lily! We've been hearing lots about you. It's lovely to meet you."

He scooped Lily into a rough hug, his beard tickling her cheek. Sam rolled her eyes.

"Papa, stop being so embarrassing."

He turned on Sam with a grin. "I'm your father. Being embarrassing is my job, young lady."

He started kissing her cheek loudly, Sam squealing and trying hard to wriggle away. Sam's dad shook his head affectionately and turned his attention back to Lily.

"Ignore them, Lily. You'll soon learn we're all mad here. Would you like to join—"

He was cut off again as an enormous golden retriever bounded into the hallway, drawn by Sam's yells. Sam's dad was bowled into her papa and the three of them fell in a tangle. The dog leapt into the pile, enthusiastically licking whichever face he could get closest to. Sam spluttered.

"Costello! You ridiculous furball, get *off*."

Costello clambered over to Lily, pushing his wet nose into her hand, tail thumping happily. Sam's papa clambered back to his feet, hoisting his husband and daughter up with him.

"Lily," said Sam's dad at last. "Do you like lasagne?"

The dinner table proved to be only slightly less riotous than the hallway. The addition of Sam's twin brothers kicked the noise levels up another few notches and Lily started to understand why Sam talked so much.

"And then she said—"

"Oh, here we go—"

"This is just like—"

"Don't get him started—"

"It's nothing like—"

"It is!"

The whole family talked constantly, yelling over each other, gesticulating wildly, laughing with their heads thrown back and their mouths full. A fine golden thread of private jokes ran through the conversation, and more than once Lily lost her grasp on it. She didn't care. She loved it.

"I was speaking to your mum earlier, Lily," said Sam's dad with a warm smile. "Brilliant woman."

Lily wrinkled her nose. "I guess. She's just my mum."

Sam's dad laughed. "Well, she seems to have settled in wonderfully. How are you liking Edge?"

"Yeah, Lily," said Sam through a mouthful of lasagne. "Why don't you tell my dad what you were saying earlier?"

Lily kicked Sam under the table. "It has its moments."

Sam boggled her eyes exaggeratedly at Lily. Lily stuck her tongue out and bit back a smile.

Costello padded around under the table, laying his head in whichever lap he thought most likely to give him food. Lily scratched his ears and slipped him a piece of bread, grinning when he licked her palm. Sam's papa reached across the table, piling plates high with seconds and thirds, even as Lily insisted she couldn't possibly eat any more. Sam winked at her across the table.

"Right, that's enough of all of you. You're scaring the life out of poor Lily. Come on, Lily, let's go upstairs."

They pushed back their chairs and headed for the stairs, leaving Sam's dads good-naturedly squabbling about whose turn it was to do the dishes.

Sam's room was exactly like Sam: a glorious mess. The back of her door was covered in photographs. Her desk was scattered with seashells and nail polish and pens. Books were stacked high on her bedside table, a jar of wilting daisies balanced precariously on top. A set of wind chimes sang in the window. Sam clicked the door shut behind her, muffling the noise from downstairs just a little.

"Sorry about them. They're—"

"They're wonderful," interrupted Lily.

Sam grinned, ducking her head sheepishly. "They're all right."

Lily wandered over to the window. "Look, you can see right into my bedroom from here."

"Creep," said Sam, grinning.

Lily dug her in the ribs. In comparison with the riot of colour in Sam's room, Lily's own room almost looked neat. She could see her colourful bedspread, piled with books, her enormous world map pinned on the wall. She glanced back over at Sam. She'd like to show it to her, to tell her how she was going to travel to every single country, having glorious adventures.

Sam kicked a pile of shoes under her bed and sat cross-legged on the rug. Lily dropped down beside her. She looked deep in thought.

"You OK?" Lily said.

Sam nodded. "I was just thinking that you should

come and meet Jay. He's really cool; you'll like him a lot. Don't tell him I said that, though." She smiled.

Lily snorted. "OK. That sounds good."

"I was thinking we could tell him about the museum. Get an extra brain in on it. But only if you want to."

Lily chewed her lip. Jealousy flared through her. It had only been their secret for a few hours and now Sam wanted to tell someone else. Sam glanced over anxiously.

"You obviously don't have to make your mind up now. Come and meet him first and then you can decide."

Lily stretched a smile on to her face and nodded. She'd meet him first and then she'd decide. Maybe he'd surprise her, she thought bitterly.

Eight

Emily was sitting by a rock pool feeding the sea anemones. She had always loved the anemones – their bright colours in the murk of the pools, their reaching tentacles blooming like alien flowers. She had some biscuits in her pocket and was crumbling them slowly into the water, watching the anemones catch the falling crumbs. You could touch them when they were out like this, feel the difference between their firm jelly bodies and the prickle of stings so tiny, they felt more sticky than sharp. Too hard a poke and they'd retreat back into themselves, but they didn't mind a little gentle probing.

She brushed the final crumbs of biscuit from her fingers and bent to look in her bucket. She had collected a little pile of whelks from the rocks. They looked like empty seashells when she first picked them up, the small animals within tucked away from her prying fingers. But, left alone for a while, they had started industriously climbing the walls of the bucket, making their way slowly back towards their homes. She had named all of them.

It was cold and the beach was almost deserted. The wind whistled in Emily's ears and slapped her cheeks to a vivid red but she hardly noticed. She liked being outside and she loved being by the sea. She was sure she could feel the histories and the stories vibrating under the sand, hiding just beneath the silver surface of the water.

She should have been afraid of the sea, after what had happened. In fact, it felt more like home than ever. Her mother loved the sea and had instilled the same love in Caitlyn and Emily. One of the clumsiest women Emily had ever seen on land, she moved with astonishing grace in the water – as though that was where she truly belonged. Emily had started to imagine that her mother had been a selkie, shedding her true form to walk on land like a human but always belonging to the sea. In these daydreams, her mother had simply returned to her real home and was still living somewhere down there. Maybe she would even come back to visit sometime.

Emily scratched a message into the sand with a

stick and watched as the waves washed it away. She hoped they'd carry it to her mother, wherever she was.

When her fingers started to go numb, she stood up. Her knees creaked in the cold. She released the whelks back into the rock pool and watched the anemones protectively draw in their tentacles, sensing the disturbance in the water.

She took the long way home. Caitlyn was trying to be brave for both of them but Emily wasn't in any hurry to face her pale, drawn face and red eyes. She clambered up the craggy rocks separating the beach from the town, giving the old lighthouse a wave in the distance.

It was completely abandoned now, the door mossed shut, the bricks loose and crumbling, the glass fogged with dirt and sea spatter. But sometimes, with the sun hitting it just right, Emily could see exactly what it must have looked like – its long, powerful searchlight swinging around to illuminate the dark sea, to guide troubled sailors to safety.

Tears took her by surprise, rising suddenly in her

throat until she tasted salt on her lips. They tasted like the sea. She scrubbed at her face with the sleeve of her jacket and sniffed heavily. She turned her back on the lighthouse and continued on her way home.

The rocks of the beach gave way to unruly beach grass, studded with the same flowers that poked out from the rock face. A trail had been beaten through, grass flattened by years of footfall, and every so often a paving slab appeared, seemingly at random. Eventually the slabs joined into a crooked path that led along the beachfront towards Emily's house.

As she approached, Emily could see Caitlyn standing in the kitchen window staring out at the sea. She raised a hand to wave to her sister but froze when Caitlyn turned to speak to someone just out of sight. She looked angry.

Emily ducked behind the garden wall, peering over into her kitchen. She still couldn't see who Caitlyn was talking to, but her sister looked frantic now. Emily could hear the insistent din of Caitlyn's shout, even through the closed window.

The front door opened and Emily ducked down

further. As she heard it swing closed, she risked a glance over. A man she'd never seen before had emerged. He cleared his throat noisily and spat on the grass. Cold anger flushed through Emily.

He was tall – taller than he originally appeared, thanks to a pronounced slouch. His face was shadowed with dark stubble, matching hair that fell scruffily towards his eyes. A crack echoed through the air as Caitlyn threw a plate into the sink. The man didn't flinch at the sound, leaning on the front gate and lighting a cigarette. He blew out a long trail of foul-smelling smoke, cleared his throat again and set off towards a car that sat empty at the side of the road.

Through the window, Emily watched her sister put her head in her soapy hands and start to cry.

Nine

To her great annoyance, Lily found that she liked Jay a whole lot, just as Sam had said she would. Eyes so dark you couldn't tell where his pupils ended and his irises began gave his face a sombre, serious look. Everything about him was neat, from his spotless school uniform to his neat rows of braids, standing him in glorious contrast to Sam's chaos.

He had a quiet, biting sense of humour, which meant that it would often be a few minutes before anyone realised he had said anything funny. Even in bed with the flu, mischief sparked just under his skin and Lily found herself telling him all about the Museum of Emily, spurred on by his excitement and curiosity.

The three of them talked of nothing else as they walked to school together on Monday morning, Lily getting caught up and waving her arms around as they bounced theories and questions off each other. She turned stubbornly away from Ms Hanan's triumphant face as they entered her classroom still talking.

What they needed, they decided, was a base. Somewhere they could collect everything that they knew about Emily and her museum, and all the clues they would surely find. Ideally, somewhere with a great big pinboard, like in a detective story, with different-coloured string connecting mysterious photographs and scraps of paper from which the big picture would eventually, undoubtedly, appear.

Jay shared a room with his older brother, so his house was out. Sam technically had her own room but her family were always wandering in and out. Lily loved being at Sam's house, and had found plenty of excuses to drop by since her first dinner there. But as a base it was a no-go too.

Lily's own house was the opposite, which somehow presented exactly the same problem. When there were only two of you in the house, it was pretty hard to hide anything. The house was quiet and whispered secrets would carry. Besides, since the move, Lily's mum had been "taking an active interest" in everything her daughter did. In theory, very nice. In reality, quite annoying sometimes.

Jay had the idea of the school newspaper. They would go to the headmistress, Ms Bruce, and claim that they wanted to restart the school newspaper. They would get resources, a safe base and a great excuse to hang out together after school without anyone getting suspicious. It was a brilliant plan, with one fatal flaw. Ms Bruce was a tyrant.

The headmistress was one of those people who viewed all children merely as short, inferior, irritating adults, who should be encouraged to grow up as quickly as possible. She seemed to have become a teacher with the sole purpose of throwing her weight around and squashing childish notions like imagination and fun as efficiently and entirely as she could.

Ms Bruce hated Sam. Sam talked too much and too loudly, her hair was always in a tangle and, more often than not, she had food spilled down her front – generally because she refused to stop talking, even when her mouth was full. She was *improper*, the worst thing a girl could be. Lily was improper by association. It was only thanks to Jay that they made it into her office at all. Like many adults, Ms Bruce mistook his quietness for meekness.

Even though they had requested the meeting, Lily still felt as though she was in trouble. Everything in the headmistress's office seemed designed to make her feel small and afraid. In fact, when Lily bent to retrieve a pen that had fallen out of her pocket as she sat down, she noticed that the headmistress's chair was unusually tall. It meant that Ms Bruce seemed to tower over her – but under the desk, her feet dangled in the air like a child's. Lily disguised her delighted giggle as a cough.

Ms Bruce had an elastic, fishy sort of face, perpetually set to disapproval. The corners of her mouth stretched to improbable proportions as she explained that running a school newspaper would serve only as a *distraction* from their studies and that people who ran newspapers generally *lacked character*. Ms Bruce was very big on character. She sensed Sam gearing up for a speech on the freedom of the press, and unceremoniously turfed them out of her office.

With all her outrage unspent, Sam continued working herself into a rage all the way along the corridor. In an attempt to defuse her, Lily told them about the modified chair. They blinked at her in unison, before dissolving into helpless giggles.

"She is ridiculous," howled Sam. "We should sneak in and lop a few inches off."

"Or swap the chairs," said Jay. "See how she likes it when we're suddenly towering over her."

They leaned against the walls, chuckling weakly.

"OK, so no newspaper," said Lily.

"I suppose that *was* a long shot," said Jay.

"What do we do now?" said Sam.

"For now, we go old-school. Keep everything we know in notebooks and carry them with us," said Lily.

"Should be easy; we don't know anything yet," said Jay.

"True. Shall we head to the library after school? See if we can find something?"

Once they got to the library, they set up in the

basement and resumed the tedious business of leafing through the town records. This time, though, it took less than an hour to strike gold. Lily almost tore the page from the record book in her excitement.

"I have one! I have one! A Joanie McCrae died in Edge about twenty years ago."

Sam and Jay crowded round her. When she saw the name, Sam pulled the two into an excited embrace and jumped up and down. Lily felt warmth spread in her stomach again, tempered by the slight worry that Sam might pull her head off.

She shook them off with a laugh and sent Sam to find the newspapers from the matching year, in case there was anything about the death in there. They lifted the box to the table and spread the papers across its huge surface.

Jay spotted it. "Look, here! Local woman dies in tragic boating accident."

Lily took the paper from him. "She was only forty when she died. That's so awful."

"Does she have anything to do with our Emily?"

"Not sure. A proficient sailor … boat discovered

wrecked in the harbour ... no body found ... survived by her two daughters, aged eleven and seventeen. No names for the daughters. I guess they probably weren't allowed to name them."

"We need to find out who they were. It looks as though they could have been the most recent McCraes."

Subtracting from the date of the newspaper article, Lily and Jay took a box each and started searching for the daughters' birth records. Sam, who was almost as precious with the library as Ms Bright, frantically tried to restore order to the chaotic table.

"I can't believe it! I've *found* her!" yelled Jay, forgetting to keep his voice down. "It's definitely her. Joanie McCrae was Emily's mother."

The three turned back to the newspaper, where Joanie McCrae smiled vibrantly, oblivious to the troubles in her future. The other people in the photograph had been cropped out but on the right-hand side by Joanie's hip was a pair of small, serious eyes. Lily felt goosebumps rise on her arms again.

"Emily," she murmured.

The sadness of the story muted their victory a little, but they were still bubbling over by the time they re-emerged in the main library.

"What are you three cooking up down there?" said Ms Bright, grinning at their infectious enthusiasm.

"School project, Ms Bright," said Jay. "Too many distractions at home. We get loads more done here."

"Well, just since it's you three, if you ever need study space you can always borrow one of the reading rooms."

"The what?"

The reading rooms were tucked down the back of the basement. Each contained a small round desk, four chairs, a sofa and three shelves. One wall was covered in chalkboard paint. The opposite, to Lily's absolute delight, housed an enormous pinboard. The three exchanged glances, barely able to contain their excitement.

"Oh, Ms Bright, it's *perfect*," said Lily. "Could we borrow it? Just for a while?"

"Of course you can. The key hangs on a little hook

behind the desk. It's the one with a green ribbon. Just ask anytime, or grab it yourself if I'm not around."

They spilled out of the library, buoyed almost to hysteria by their double triumph. They had the start of Emily's story and a place to work out the rest. It felt like it was only a matter of time before the puzzle started to fit together.

Lily suddenly felt the hairs on the back of her neck prick up. She spun, peering into the evening shadows, sure that someone was watching them. The street was empty. There was nothing. Just an uneasy feeling and the faint, unpleasant tang of cigarette smoke hanging in the air.

Ten

Emily had tried to ask Caitlyn about the sinister man but Caitlyn had brushed her off. She had prodded and poked, hearing herself getting annoying, until eventually Caitlyn had snapped and demanded to be left alone. They didn't speak for a few hours.

After a while, Caitlyn reappeared and apologised. She insisted that she was just tired, and arranged her face in a false, forced brightness that made Emily's insides hurt to look at. Emily grabbed her raincoat from the coat hook and ran out of the house, shouting a goodbye.

She drifted around the quiet streets of her town, pulling her coat tight against the hungry wind, kicking pebbles along the main street, almost relishing the depths of her gloom. She was jerked out of her hazy state by a familiar and entirely unwelcome smell. The rich, tarry scent of cigarette smoke was weaving its way towards her. She tried to ignore her shaking hands and stuffed them crossly into her pockets. Lots of people smoked.

But it was him. The same man she'd seen leave their house. He slunk round a corner at the far edge of the street. Emily stepped back and pressed herself against a wall, hoping that it might give way and hide her somehow. She dug her nails into her palms, half wanting to march up to him and demand to know what he'd done to her sister. But fear pricked her, cold and insistent. She knew that you couldn't judge a person based on what they looked like. She knew that. But still. Silly or not, he didn't look good.

Panic squirted in her mouth as he suddenly locked eyes with her. Recognition flickered across his face and he frowned slightly, as though trying to place her. She tried to keep her face blank as she looked away and turned her back on him. She'd taken a couple of steps when she heard his voice behind her.

"Hey!"

She walked faster. Heavy footsteps followed her. She risked a quick glance behind and saw that the man was coming towards her, his hurried gait betraying the false casualness of his expression. She didn't care how silly she looked; she turned and ran.

She heard him take off after her. She threw herself round corners, feet sliding on the wet cobblestones, hoping that the town would recognise the man as an enemy and trip him.

His legs were long and he was gaining on her. She rounded another corner and looked frantically around for a place to hide. There was nothing. She had run down an alley of old fishermen's cottages, walls flat and white, making her more conspicuous than ever. Her eyes fell on one of the doors. It was slightly open and covered in grime. She pressed her eye to the gap and was rewarded with a faceful of cobwebs. She spluttered and swatted at her face. But there was one positive. It didn't look like anyone had lived there for a long time.

She threw her body against the door and for a horrifying moment it didn't move. She could hear his footsteps getting closer. Slowly, excruciatingly slowly, it started to move. She squeezed through the gap and jammed the door back to its previous almost-closed position. The man's footsteps entered the street and stopped. Emily held her breath.

"Why are you running, Emily?"

A finger of ice ran up Emily's spine at the sound of her own name. His footsteps drew closer.

"I'm not going to hurt you. I just want to talk."

It sounded like he was right outside the door. Emily backed away, lifting her feet high and putting them down gently. Her back came to rest against the metal railing of a rusted spiral staircase. The man's footsteps had stopped. Emily stood perfectly still, her ears straining into the uneasy silence.

With every second that passed, she became more convinced that he was lurking just on the other side of the door, waiting to pounce. An illogical scream rose in her chest and her skin started to prickle with goosebumps. She forced the scream back down and gripped on to the cold railing, hoping that it would ground her.

She glanced upwards. The staircase was old, no doubt about it. It was caked in rust, and cobwebs blurred the spaces between stairs. But despite its age, it looked sturdy. She put a foot on the bottom step, the creak of the metal as loud as a scream in her ears. She froze again, listening for any sounds from outside. Nothing. Slowly she made her way upwards, wincing at every scrape of her shoes against the rough surface. At least upstairs there was bound to be a cupboard she could hide in, or a window she could crawl through, in case he did come through the door.

She reached the top of the staircase and scurried for the safety of the first room. She stopped, her fear momentarily forgotten. The room she had entered was bizarre. It was completely empty, stretched long and thin, the full length of the cottage. She crept towards the door at the end and pushed. Her delight was so complete that she almost yelled aloud, forgetting that she was supposed to be hiding. Two levels were visible, stretching the length of another two houses. The cottages weren't cottages at all. It was a false front. She was standing in an old smugglers' warehouse.

Edge was full of things like this, even all these years after its more ... colourful inhabitants had died out. Secret tunnels criss-crossed the town, between houses and warehouses like this one, between the caves that riddled the cliffs on the edge of town and the sea itself. Emily was obsessed with the pirates and had dragged Caitlyn on treasure hunts through countless caves. Caitlyn normally cut those adventures short, saying she was afraid of rock slides. Emily suspected she was actually scared of the dark.

Emily made her way down to the lower level of the warehouse, peering into boxes and under cloths, just in case any treasure had been left behind. Unless mouse droppings and birds' nests had significantly risen in value since she'd entered the building, she was out of luck. The walls were solid brick; the windows outside must be fake too, but on the opposite end of the building to where she'd come in, there was a small door.

She edged the door open and put one eye to the crack. She was facing towards the sea now. She couldn't see the man. She opened the door a little more and risked poking her head out. He was gone. Emily rested her forehead against the cool surface of the door, taking deep, gulping breaths and trying to steady her heart.

Eleven

Lily, Sam and Jay had been dividing their time between their base at the library and the museum. Using the town records, Lily had been attempting to draw up Emily's family tree. Her efforts dominated the chalkboard. Despite Ms Bright's meticulous record-keeping, information on the McCraes was hard to find. It seemed as though at one time there had been lots of them. If it was the same McCrae family, they had owned the old lighthouse and been pillars of the community. A generation or two later, the tree dwindled to a single branch and then to just Emily and her family, and then to none at all. What had happened to the McCrae family – and did it have anything to do with Emily's museum? It was a question that bothered Lily like a loose tooth, and she couldn't stop prodding at it.

Jay was focused on the building that housed the museum. He trawled through town blueprints and deeds of ownership, looking for any clue as to who the mysterious museum might belong to. So far he'd had no luck at all. In fact, in every plan of the town he'd looked at, the building was drawn up as three fishermen's cottages, just as it appeared from the outside.

Sam had become fixated on Joanie McCrae's accident. She pored over newspaper cuttings and ageing weather reports, even finding an order of service for Joanie's funeral tucked inside one box of newspapers.

They took it in turns to visit the museum and catalogue the exhibits, that being by far the most fun job. Some exhibits were touched with sadness – a button from a favourite coat grown too small, a faded black-and-white photograph of a man and a woman dancing. Some made the three smile – a scribbled limerick about a teacher, a beaded friendship bracelet. Almost all were remarkable only in their unremarkableness. Some, though, caught their attention.

As the days grew shorter and the walk to and from the museum grew colder, Sam's reluctance to touch the exhibits faltered and faded. Rather than running to the library to fetch her friends and returning to the museum, she conceded that interesting things could be brought to the library on the strict condition that they were returned exactly as they had been found.

Lily was elbow-deep in a box of marriage certificates when Sam burst into the reading room, making her and Jay jump. Her nose was pink from the cold but her eyes were shining.

"What have you got?" said Jay.

"I'm not sure. But I think it might be good."

She tugged off her scarf and sat between her friends. From her pocket she produced a small tube, which she placed ceremoniously on the table. Jay and Lily peered at it. It was smooth and black, apart from the flaky red remains of what looked like a wax seal. A seam ran down the length of the tube.

"It was the very last thing in the museum. In a case all of its own."

"What is it?" Lily asked.

"I have no idea. I haven't looked inside yet. But you want to know what the label said?"

Her friends waited. Sam leaned in and looked at the tube delightedly.

"It's a secret."

"You're not going to tell us?" said Jay.

Sam rolled her eyes extravagantly. "No, you clot, that's what the label said. That's what this is. It's a secret."

Lily blinked at her, her face splitting into a wide grin. "I can't believe you didn't open it. I wouldn't have been able to resist."

Sam matched her grin. "Shall we look?"

"Yes! Open it, the suspense is killing me," laughed Jay.

Sam ran a finger along the seam, finding where the tube came apart. It popped open, expelling a puff of musty air and a scrap of yellowed paper, tightly rolled. She took a deep breath and flattened the paper on the table. They crowded round to read.

X marks the spot.

"X marks the spot?" Lily snatched up the piece of paper and turned it over, at exactly the same time that Jay grabbed the tube and peered inside

for another page.

"It's like..." She faded out, not wanting to sound stupid.

"Like a treasure hunt," finished Sam.

"Not much use without a map, though. How are we supposed to find the X?" said Jay.

"Maybe we're not supposed to find it. The label did say it was a secret," said Sam.

"Perhaps there's a map hidden somewhere else in Emily's museum," said Lily.

"You mean the Museum of Emily?" Jay was looking at her curiously.

"That's what I said."

"You didn't. You said 'Emily's museum'. Like Emily was the one who made it."

"Do you think she did?" asked Sam.

"I ... I don't know. I don't know what I think."

"I think we need to go back to the museum and look. All of us. This is our best clue so far."

When they got outside it was dark, the streets eerie and unfamiliar in the dusk.

"What time is it?" asked Lily.

Jay looked at his watch and winced. "My mum will freak out if I'm not home for dinner again. Sam, she keeps hassling me about seeing you. Do you want to come over?"

"Sure! Lily, how about you? There's always food at Jay's; his mum always makes too much."

"Nah, better not. My mum keeps making jokes about how she doesn't recognise me any more. I think I'd better go and hang out with her for a bit."

There had been a lot of family dinners missed in the pursuit of this "school project". Lily waved goodbye to her friends and stepped out of the golden circle of light at the library door, wrapping her scarf tightly around her face. The nights were getting cold and Lily was glad to see the glow of her little house winking at the end of the road.

The warmth inside made her eyelids droop. She dragged herself up to her room and scribbled the day's findings in her notebook, not stopping to care about whether her handwriting would be readable in the morning. She wrote down everything that she could remember, from the date of the accident to the pair of small serious eyes in the photograph. And at last she fell asleep, dreaming that her bed was a tiny boat, drifting and bucking lonesomely out to sea.

Twelve

Lily, Sam and Jay divided up the museum, re-examining anything that looked like it might contain a map or lead them to another clue. Lily looked at every page of the copy of *James and the Giant Peach*. Sam turned over each scrap of paper to see what was on the back. Jay scoured every scribble of Emily's handwriting, convinced that at any moment a cypher or code would become clear.

A yell from Sam brought them running. She was holding up a tiny black tube, much smaller than the one the message had come in.

"That doesn't look like a map,' said Lily.

Sam fixed her with a look. "It's a roll of film. These could be Emily's photographs."

Lily took it from her and peered at it, as though the photos would reveal themselves if she looked hard enough. "Well, what are we supposed to do with that? How do you get the photographs out?"

"You develop them in a darkroom," said Sam.

"Where are we meant to get one of those?"

Sam grinned and pulled her camera from its usual position round her neck.

"You don't!" said Lily incredulously.

"I do," said Sam. "My dad said that if I was going to be a photographer, I might as well do it properly."

Sam's darkroom was in the attic of her house. They succeeded in shaking off her dads and her brothers but Costello proved more persistent and ended up crammed in there with them. Lily, Jay and Costello were all banished to the dry side of the darkroom, housing the table, the dim red light and some expensive-looking equipment, which Sam told them not to touch on pain of death.

Meanwhile Sam installed herself on the other side of the room, carefully unwinding and winding the film, pouring chemicals that made Lily's eyes water. Eventually she crossed back over, holding the film in her fingertips and nudging them out of the way with her hip.

"We only have one shot at this, so don't touch them. Don't even breathe on them. In fact, don't even look at them too hard; you might make them shy."

She clipped them to the drying line, washed her hands and turned back to her friends, who were obediently looking away from the lines of film, sneaking glances through their eyelashes.

"And now we wait," said Sam.

"How long?"

"A couple of hours, probably."

"A couple of *hours*?" yelled Lily and Jay in unison.

"Good things come to those who wait, you philistines."

"What's a philistine?"

Sam frowned. "It's what my dad calls his manager at the theatre."

They went downstairs and poked around in the kitchen for some food. Sam made cheese sandwiches and cut slices of leftover cinnamon cake but they were too agitated to eat, pulling at the crusts of their sandwiches and crumbling pieces of cake in their hands. Even Costello seemed to be feeling the strain, pacing erratically and refusing to settle in his basket. He laid his head in Sam's lap and she fussed at his ears, letting him lick scraps of icing from her fingers. Sam's dad, who had been bustling around attempting to make conversation, eventually got fed up with them and chucked them all out of the house, including Costello.

It was a blustery day, not exactly raining, more like the air itself was wet. They walked along the beach, the wind whipping sand and salty smatterings of spray into their faces. Nevertheless, they were in high spirits. The promise of another clue made them wild and jittery with excitement. They tossed pebbles into the choppy water, threw sticks for Costello to chase, took it in turns to clamber precariously around the rock pools when Costello got overexcited and launched himself in after a crab or a piece of particularly exciting seaweed.

He hared off down the beach, ears flapping ridiculously as he went. Sam went flying after him, yelling his name to no avail. Lily laughed as she watched them, the laugh dying in her throat as she saw Costello stop in front of a man on the sand and rear backwards, ears flattened against his head. The wind carried the low growl back to her, raising the hairs on her arms.

The man reached out a hand to the dog, who ducked away and continued to growl. Sam reached them and Lily watched as her friend spoke to him, waving her hands apologetically. She hooked Costello back on to his lead and dragged him with some difficulty back towards her friends.

"Idiot dog," she said, shaking her head. "No idea what got into him. He's probably drunk on seawater or something."

"What did he say?"

"Who, the guy? He was fine. Made a joke about dogs being good judges of character."

Lily frowned and looked back across the beach, where the man was just a dark smudge against the sand. Sam ran a hand through her long hair and checked her watch.

"Let's head back. Our film might be ready by now."

Back in the darkroom, the film had changed. Shadowy images were visible on the surface and Lily's heart jumped with excitement. Sam fed the film into a complicated-looking machine and dropped sheets of paper into her chemical trays, rocking them to make the images appear.

"Hey! I do know this! I've seen this bit in movies," said Lily. "Can I have a go?"

"Absolutely not."

Lily looked over at Jay, who rolled his eyes affectionately. As she developed the prints, Sam hung them from the string and Lily felt tears prick at her eyes as she got her first glimpse of Emily's life.

Two girls in front of a tinsel-coated tree; a teenage girl running down the beach with her younger sister on her back, both of them screaming with laughter; a woman and a girl caught in the middle of an extravagant cancan dance, their legs high in the air, heads thrown back. The photos crackled with life and love, each face within so completely alive that Lily almost expected them to turn and look at her.

Sam's mouth was a solemn line as she hung photo after photo on the line, the knowledge of what had happened to this little family making the pictures desperately sad. Sam frowned as she pulled an image from her tray, holding it away from her. The image was grey and blurry. The next was the same, a thin gold line streaking down one side.

"Maybe they didn't mean to take these. Or I've done something wrong with the film."

"The others are all OK, though."

Sam touched a finger gently to the gold line. "With old film cameras, you had to wind the film on between photographs. This looks like it hasn't been properly wound. See how it's like two photos mashed together?"

"Maybe whoever took it was in a hurry."

"Or maybe they didn't know how to use the camera properly."

"It looks like there's something there. In the corner, see?"

"Hang on."

Sam clattered out of the room and returned a minute or two later, a magnifying glass clutched in her hand. They crowded around the photograph. Lily's heart froze. Sam's face creased in confusion.

"It's the man from the beach."

"Who?" said Jay.

"The man from the beach. The one that Costello was barking at earlier."

"What? Are you sure?"

"Definitely," said Lily, peering closer. "It was literally about an hour ago. It was him."

"It could be an accidental photo," said Jay.

"Some coincidence, though," said Sam.

The man looked out at them from the edge of the photo, his hand raised as if to grab something.

Thirteen

After her chase, Emily had decided to confront Caitlyn again about the man. She chose her moment carefully and waited until after dinner, knowing that Caitlyn was generally more easy-going on a full stomach. She helped with the dishes, brought Caitlyn a cup of tea and gave her a minute to settle down and relax. Then she perched on the armchair across from her sister's, poking her fingers into the holes in the patterned seat cover.

"Caitlyn?"

"Hmm?"

"Please tell me who that man was."

Annoyance flickered across Caitlyn's face, smoothed away so quickly that Emily would have missed it if she wasn't watching so closely. "What man?"

"The man who came to the house the other day. The one who upset you."

"I already told you. He was nobody and he didn't upset me."

The stubborn twist of her mouth was mirrored on Emily's face. "I saw you through the window. Crying after he left."

Caitlyn picked up a newspaper and started to leaf through it. The smile she offered Emily was watery and thin. "Sweetheart, we talked about this already. You must have been too far away to see properly. I wasn't crying. I wasn't upset. You can keep asking but that's still going to be the answer."

"So what was he doing in our house?"

"He was just some random guy doing a survey."

It was a lie. Emily couldn't remember Caitlyn lying to her before. Her temper rose, heat flushing up the back of her neck. "He knows my name."

Caitlyn froze. "He what?"

"He knows my name. He shouted at me, chased me through town. Why would some stranger do that?"

"I don't know," said Caitlyn, her voice wavering.

"Stop *lying* to me!" Emily's voice was louder than she had expected, ringing round the small living room. Caitlyn's head jerked as she flinched away from Emily's shout. She folded her newspaper, tossed it on to the coffee table and stood up.

"I think we're done talking about this for tonight."

Emily followed her into the kitchen. "We haven't even started talking about it. You're not telling me anything."

"That's because I'm handling it."

"Let me help."

"I don't need your help. I need you to stop pushing me all the time."

"No! I won't. I want you to tell me what's going on. I want you to tell me who that man was and why he made you so upset. I want you to tell me when we started having secrets from each other."

"There are some things you're too young to understand."

"I'm not a baby."

"I'm not saying that you're a baby."

"That's exactly what you're saying."

"I'm not, I—" Caitlyn blew out a long, slow breath and rubbed her hands roughly across her face. "I'm just trying to look after you."

"You don't have to look after me. Stop pretending

that you're so much more grown-up than I am. You're not Mum."

The words landed like a slap. Shame bleached through Emily as the colour drained from Caitlyn's face. The silence ringing around the room seemed to stretch for hours, days.

Caitlyn turned away and Emily saw her shoulders start to shake. She wiped her eyes fiercely and pushed past Emily out of the room. Emily reached out a hand towards her sister as she passed, but Caitlyn spun and slapped it away.

"*Don't,*" she hissed. Her footsteps faded up the stairs and her bedroom door slammed, shaking every window in the house.

Emily stood breathing heavily, shock still hitting her in waves. Why had she said that? She poured herself a cup of cold water and drank hungrily, her teeth chattering against the glass, water spilling down her front.

She knew exactly why she had said it. She had wanted to hurt Caitlyn. She was upset and angry that Caitlyn was keeping a secret, so she had picked the cruellest words she could muster and thrown them with all her strength. She felt sick. She had no idea how she was going to fix this. It was dark outside and the kitchen window showed her reflection in sharp focus. She glared into her own eyes accusingly.

Suddenly she was seized with the uneasy thought that someone could be standing on the other side of the window, cloaked by the darkness, watching her. Sick, irrational panic pooled in her stomach and she flicked the light switch down hard, pitching the kitchen into darkness.

She stared out of the window, letting her eyes adjust and start to make out shapes in the garden outside. A flicker of movement drew her gaze but it was just the bushes blowing in the wind. Suddenly exhausted, she swiped at her eyes and made her way upstairs to bed. If she had been less tired, maybe she would have noticed what might have been a shadow slowly moving through the garden away from her.

Less than a week after their fight, Emily and Caitlyn McCrae disappeared.

Fourteen

The mystery man's appearance in the photograph had given Lily and her friends a new lead to follow. Sam had taken to dragging poor Costello all around the town in the hope that he might sniff out their elusive villain. What exactly she was planning to do if they found him, no one was really sure. They pinned the blurry photograph right in the middle of their pinboard, a great big question mark beside it.

Both the pinboard and their chalkboard were filling up, more with questions than answers. Lily's family tree had stalled. The branches that didn't end with Emily and her sister led out of Edge and so were proving hard to track down.

Having studied town-planning records until he was cross-eyed, Jay was working on sketching a map of the town, marking out places connected to the McCrae family and anything else he found interesting. Lily had been hugely excited at the discovery of the warren of secret tunnels criss-crossing the town, until her friends rolled their eyes and told her that *everyone* knew about them.

Jay's map was enormous and beautiful, taking up the majority of their table, meaning that piles of notepads and various papers had now moved to the floor. Lily followed the roads with her fingertips, affectionately circling their three houses, where Jay had sketched them in cartoon, Sam holding up a camera, him gripping a pencil, Lily peeking over a tottering pile of books.

When they started to feel stir crazy, they'd go to the beach, letting the cold air blow away the cobwebs. They were sitting on the crumbling wall of the promenade, trying to ignore the fact that it was raining into their chips. Lily warmed her hands on the paper bag, impatiently popping chips into her mouth and rolling them around to stop them burning her. The salt stung her lips. She realised that it tasted like the sea, and that the sea was starting to taste like home. Sam reached over and stole a handful of chips, cramming them all into her mouth at once.

"I think we need to go back to the note," she said around a mouthful of potato. "It still feels like the key to me."

"I don't know," said Lily. "X marks the spot? It's not exactly very specific. It's the clue to every treasure map ever. It was probably part of a game or something like that."

Sam shook her head. "No way. Remember what the label said. Whatever that note was, it was important enough to be a secret."

"OK. So if it's a treasure map sort of a clue, maybe we need to go back and try treasure map sort of techniques. Look for codes again. Or invisible ink."

"How do you find invisible ink?"

Lily sucked salt from her fingers. "Lemon juice. Or a UV light."

"We can't pour lemon juice all over a twenty-year-old clue. What if it dissolves?"

Lily shrugged. "Then I guess we'd have nothing."

She fed Costello a chip. He settled his head contentedly on her knees.

They headed back towards the library, dropping Costello off at Sam's house on the way. Ms Bright liked them, but she didn't like them *that* much.

Lily pushed open the door of their reading room and the breath was punched from her lungs. The room had been completely trashed. Papers had been ripped from their pinboard and strewn across the floor, coloured threads left hanging loose. Chalky handprints were smeared across the blackboard. An enormous gash had been cut through the middle of Jay's map. The photograph of the man was gone.

Sam stood by the table, running a finger along the slit in Jay's map, horror dawning slowly on her face. Jay's dark skin was ashy and tight-looking. Lily looked in panic from one to the other, waiting for one of them to say something brave, crack a joke, anything to distract from the sound of her own stupid, terrified heart hammering in her ears. Sam opened and closed her mouth a couple of times, shaking her head.

"Who could have done this?"

"Anyone could go behind the desk and get the key if they knew it was there," said Jay, his voice shaking.

"Does this mean that someone's been watching us?"

When she spoke, Lily's voice was high and hysterical, horribly, falsely carefree. "Well, who cares if someone has been? That's what you sign up for with a mystery like this, right?"

Sam and Jay blinked at her, identical baffled looks on their faces.

"Are you crazy?" said Sam. "We can't keep going."

Lily's heart thunked in her chest. The museum was the whole reason Sam and Jay were here. The mystery was what was holding the three of them together.

"What do you mean? Of course we can."

"Look at Jay's map," said Sam, pointing to the huge gash. "Someone doesn't want us looking into this and that someone has a knife."

"But we've got to keep looking."

"No, Lily, we don't," said Jay.

They were ganging up on her. The two of them together, just like before she'd arrived.

"Seriously? We're just giving up?"

"You can't give up something you never had. All we have here is a big load of nothing. We've been poking around for weeks and getting nowhere. Maybe that's because there's nothing to find."

Lily flushed hot. Maybe they'd been looking for an excuse to bail this whole time.

"You've got to be kidding me. Look at this place. Someone did this because we're getting close to something. Maybe something big. Someone did this because they're scared."

"*I'm* scared."

Lily looked between them, aghast. Jay shook his head sadly at her. Ice pounded in her veins. Her friends were meant to make her better, stronger. If they were going to be such cowards, she didn't want to be friends with them either. Anger coiled in her stomach, prickling at her skin.

"But you're not supposed to be scared."

"Oh, we're not *supposed* to be scared? Well, why didn't you say so before? Now I feel loads better. We're not characters in one of your stupid stories, Lily. You don't get to decide how we're *supposed* to feel."

"Fine, go! Give up. I don't want you here anyway. You're boring and nothing, just like this town is boring and nothing, just like I knew you would be. You don't deserve a mystery like this."

She refused to see the hurt seeping into Sam's eyes or the way Jay's mouth tightened as she yelled. She hated them.

Sam opened her mouth as if she was going to say something, but then she just turned and marched out in a swirl of tartan coat and tangled, shiny hair. Lily turned to Jay, her arms folded.

He held her gaze for a moment and then pushed past, leaving her alone in the wreckage of the reading room.

Fifteen

On Monday morning Sam wasn't waiting at Lily's gate. She and Jay turned away as Lily came into the classroom, keeping their eyes down as she slid into the desk behind them. Lily furiously swiped at the tear that dropped on to her desk. She wasn't upset. She had been fine on her own before and she'd be fine on her own now. Even better without them distracting her. She'd solve the mystery of Emily all by herself and then they'd be sorry. Her chest contracted as Jay whispered something to Sam, sending her laugh spiralling into the air. She brought her lunch to Ms Hanan's classroom. Ms Hanan raised an eyebrow enquiringly, rushing over and taking Lily's hand when she put her head on the desk and started to cry.

On the way home she barged past Sam's house, half hoping someone would see her, mostly dreading that they might. But only Costello came to greet her, bounding over merrily and pushing his face over the top of the wall. As she marched past, he started to whine. Huffing out a huge sigh, she turned and petted his silky ears. He hadn't done anything wrong, after all.

In her room, she turned her photograph of the three of them down on its face, before stuffing it in a drawer for good measure.

As autumn continued its unstoppable slide towards winter, Edge grew cold and hard. The sky sat heavy and leaden on top of the town, the streets rang with sheets of ice, the grey sea looked sharp enough to cut. The sun sagged low in the sky, as though it was too tired to go any further, throwing the town into a near constant dusk.

Lily returned to the library. She binned anything the vandal had destroyed, stuffed anything that could be salvaged into her satchel and handed the key back to Ms Bright, telling her that they wouldn't be needing the room any more; that the project was over. Sam must have told her about their fight because she didn't look surprised.

Her bag filled with all their research, she decided

to go home via the museum. She would be braver than her friends. She should probably stop thinking of them like that, now that they weren't friends any more. She ignored the sick feeling in her stomach as she made her way through the darkening streets. It was even darker in the alleys, the houses crammed so close together that the weak sunlight hardly penetrated at all. Lily walked quickly, irrationally certain that something was just behind her, snapping at her heels, ready to pounce the second she turned round. She forced herself to slow down. She was fine. She wasn't scared.

The streets were quiet, the cold having driven everyone into their houses. Her footsteps echoed on the frozen cobbles, a scuffling rhythm following a split second after her steps. She stopped. So did the sound of her footsteps. Or had there been the sound of a footstep after she had stopped?

She turned and looked back up the lane. A shadow by the wall stirred and she found her path blocked by a man. Lily's heart thunked in her chest. It was him. The man from the beach. The man from

Emily's photographs. His face was lit briefly as he struck a match and lit his cigarette, then it quickly faded back into the gloom. He blew a long stream of smoke into Lily's face. She struggled to hold in a cough, not wanting to give him the satisfaction.

"Can I help you?" she said, squaring her shoulders and tilting her chin at him.

He smiled unpleasantly. "I hear you're interested in the McCrae girl."

Lily felt cold. "I don't know what you're talking about."

The man laughed, coughed and spat a yellow mass into the street. Lily wrinkled her nose.

"You and your little friends shouldn't talk so loud if you want to keep secrets."

"What do you care?"

"Oh, I'm an old friend, that's all. Haven't seen her in a long time. Would be good to catch up."

"We don't know where she is." It was the truth, after all.

"Don't lie to me, little girl. Next time you see her, you tell her Horace Snyde says hello. Tell her I haven't forgotten about her."

Fear rose metallic in Lily's throat. Snyde didn't wait for her answer, just crunched his match under his heel and stalked off.

Lily stood breathing hard. She couldn't see him any more but she couldn't shake the thought that he was lurking in the shadows, waiting to see what she did next. Whoever Snyde was, he seemed to want to hurt Emily. And the key to finding Emily was in that museum, Lily was sure of it. She had to protect her.

Decisively, she veered away from the road leading to the museum, zigzagging back towards her house. She kicked off her boots in the hall, locking the front door behind her, just in case.

The house was empty, so Lily dragged her satchel through to the kitchen and made herself a peanut butter sandwich. She'd need all her strength to go through all their notes again. There was a note from her mum stuck to the fridge and Lily skimmed it quickly. She almost dropped her sandwich.

Gone to shops at the X. Back soon.

She tore the note from the fridge and stared at it, as though that would reveal some hidden information. At the sound of her mum's key in the door, Lily bounded to meet her, almost bowling her over in the process. Lily's mum disentangled herself from her daughter, heaving her shopping bags on to the table and shaking tiny snowflakes from her hair.

Lily waved the note at her. "What does this mean?"

Her mum blinked at her. "It means I went shopping. What's got into you?"

"But what does it mean? Where did you go?"

Lily's mum pointed to the note in Lily's hand. "What are you talking about? I went to the cross."

The cross. The main junction in Edge, if you could even call it that. Two roads, cutting perpendicular to each other, shops on each side. A giant X. Surely it couldn't be that simple?

Sixteen

Lily woke up early to go to the cross. Edge was quiet as usual, shop owners hanging awnings and polishing their signs for the day ahead, a few sleepy-looking office workers sipping coffee, a young woman walking her dog, still wearing her pyjamas. A fine mist hung over everything, sparkling in the cold, settling in salty waves on Lily's skin. She glanced both ways and walked into the road. In the middle of the crossroads was a gold engraving of a compass. Lily had walked over it a hundred times, never really noticing it.

Arrows stretched in the four directions from an intricate centre circle, letters moulded elegantly into their points. From above, it really was like a huge golden X in the middle of town. Instinct tugged at Lily, sending prickles from the soles of her feet all the way to her scalp. There was something here. She could feel it. She walked around the compass, looking for anything out of the ordinary. Her breath hitched. Just above the E, someone had scratched a tiny heart. E for East. E for Emily.

She ran, drawing irate beeps from cars as she ploughed excitedly along the road. She reached the end of her road and looked both ways. She had instinctively been running for Sam, but the memory of Sam's furious face stopped her in her tracks. She turned towards Jay's. For now, that felt like the safer choice.

She banged on the door, only remembering as she heard someone grumble behind it just how early it was. The door opened and Jay glared at her, his eyes still half shut. He was wearing his pyjamas, his face rumpled with sleep, so at odds with his usual tidiness that Lily almost laughed. Until she remembered they were still in a fight.

"Do you have any idea what time it is? I'm going to report you for antisocial behaviour."

It was a better reaction than she had been expecting. She leaned towards him.

"Jay, I think I have something."

He sighed and squinted unhappily at her. For a moment she thought he was going to shut the door in her face. Then he stepped back and gestured inside.

"You'd better come in. We're having breakfast. Take off your shoes."

She kicked off her boots and followed Jay into his kitchen. Sam had been right about Jay's mum. There was enough food laid out on the counter to feed the entire town if they decided to stop by.

"Mama, this is my friend Lily."

If Jay's mother was surprised or annoyed at having a stranger show up on her doorstep first thing in the morning, she hid it well. She fixed Lily with a radiant smile and grasped her hand warmly.

"It's lovely to meet you, Lily. Are you hungry?"

Lily's stomach answered for her, growling loudly. She flushed but Jay's mum threw back her head and laughed, clapping her hands.

"Excellent. Pull up a chair and let's get some breakfast in us. I assume whatever has brought you here at this time in the morning must be important but I promise, everything makes more sense on a full stomach."

Lily didn't argue, tucking into the enormous pile of pancakes in front of her with great enthusiasm. Jay, having eaten and woken up a little, suddenly seemed to realise that he was sitting in his pyjamas and excused himself with an embarrassed smile. Jay's mum turned her full attention to Lily, a cup of coffee steaming between her fingers.

"So what brings you to my door at this hour, Lily? Must be something exciting."

"Oh. Nothing too exciting. Just some ... school work."

"Ah yes, the mysterious school project I've been hearing so much about. It must be very interesting to have you thinking about it this early at the weekend. You and Jay have certainly been spending lots of time on it together."

She gave Lily a knowing look that made her want to crawl under the table and die. Jay came clattering back down the stairs in jeans and a plaid shirt.

"Nice shirt," said his mum, winking at Lily.

Lily felt the colour rush to her face and suddenly found her own fingernails incredibly interesting. Jay shoved a slice of toast between his teeth and motioned for Lily to follow him out. She waved a shy goodbye to his mum and followed, grateful for the burst of cold air on her hot face.

They took their familiar route down to the beach and Lily was annoyed by how much like home it felt. Jay shoved his hands deep into his pockets.

"So. Did she ask if you were my girlfriend?"

Relieved laughter burst from Lily's chest. "Yes! Well, sort of. She kind of danced round it."

Jay rolled his eyes. "Honestly, she's a nightmare. She does it with Sam all the time."

"Oh, thank goodness. I thought... Well, I don't know what I thought. I like you but I don't *like you* like you, you know?"

"I know. I don't like you like you either."

Lily smiled. "Good. We can just stay friends then."

She said it without really thinking about it. Jay fell silent, scuffing his feet as he walked. Lily tugged at a strand of hair, wrapping it round and round her finger.

"I'm sorry!" she blurted. Jay looked up at her, his eyes deep and unfathomable. "I'm sorry about what I said. I don't even know how to explain. I was angry and horrible and I'm just ... really sorry."

Jay was silent for a moment, considering. Then he gave her the ghost of a smile. She felt her insides thaw.

"So you're sorry then?"

Lily laughed. "*Really* sorry."

He nodded. "OK. Let's go and get Sam."

Seventeen

Lily's stomach was full of butterflies as they stood on Sam's doorstep. Sam might just slam the door in her face after what she'd said. She could hear Costello scuffling around inside but it took what felt like forever for the door to actually open. Sam's papa beamed when he saw them.

"Lily! It feels like we haven't seen you in forever. Come in! And, Jay, good to see you, sir."

He was wearing an elaborately patterned knitted jumper, and when Lily and Jay followed him into the living room they saw that Sam's other dad was wearing exactly the same one. He saw them looking and winked.

"We've decided to crack out our Christmas jumpers. We were feeling festive."

"It's November," said Lily.

"Exactly."

The door opened with a crash and Sam bounded in, wearing an endearingly hideous maroon jumper with a huge knitted penguin on it.

"Tah-dah!" she yelled, before her eyes fell on Jay and Lily. "Oh. Hello."

There was an awkward silence. Sam's dads exchanged a look.

"Shall we just... Yes, we'll just be... Shout if you need us." They slipped out, closing the door behind them.

Sam turned to Jay and Lily, her arms folded, her face impassive. The cheery penguin on her chest made her only slightly less intimidating.

"What do you want?" She wasn't going to make this easy.

Lily dropped her gaze to her fingers. "I wanted to say that I'm sorry."

"Sorry for what?"

"For all the things I said. I was upset and stupid and I was angry that I was scared and I was angry that you were scared because you were supposed to make me brave."

Sam blew a strand of hair upwards out of her face. "Lily ... I can't make you anything."

"I know."

"Especially not considering how boring and awful I apparently am."

"I didn't mean that. I don't think you're boring at all. I think you're..." Her voice trailed off in embarrassment. "I haven't really had friends like you before. I think you're really good."

Sam's eyes sparked, just a little. She pursed her lips and picked a thread from her jumper. "I assume you're here about Emily."

Lily nodded. "I think I have something. I think I know where the X is."

Without a word, Sam shook her head and walked out of the room. Lily's chest caved. She looked up at Jay, crestfallen. He offered a sympathetic smile and opened his mouth to say something comforting.

Sam poked her head back round the door. She had her coat on.

"Well? Aren't you two coming?"

The early-morning sunshine warmed Lily's back through her heavy winter coat and, scrabbling to keep up with Sam's long, purposeful strides, she wasn't sure she'd ever felt so happy. They made their way to the cross and as they approached, Sam's eyes lit up.

"X marks the spot. Lily, you little genius." She put an arm round Lily and jiggled her excitedly. "I must have walked over this crossroads about a billion times. How could I not see it?"

"Needed a fresh pair of eyes," said Jay, grinning at Lily.

"Look, this is why I think I'm right." She bent and pointed to the tiny heart by the E.

"OK, so if this is X, what next? Is the next clue buried under the crossroads?" said Jay.

"Well, call me crazy but I thought we could follow the massive golden arrow." Lily pointed due east, towards the sea glinting in the distance.

Sam burst out laughing. "I missed you."

Lily turned away so no one would see her grin.

They followed the road all the way to the sea, keeping an eye out for anything unusual. On the promenade was a row of benches, facing out towards the view. Lily frowned and walked round the front of the benches, looking back at their arrow.

Sure enough, the arrow pointed straight at one of them.

Sam and Jay realised what she was looking at and rounded the bench to stand beside her. Sam bent to rub dirt from the brass dedication plaque on the bench.

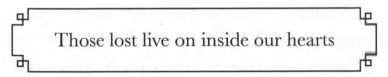

Those lost live on inside our hearts

"Mean anything to anyone?" asked Lily.

Sam shrugged. "It just sounds like every other dedication ever."

"It sounds sort of religious. Living on and all that. Maybe the next clue is in a church? Or a graveyard?" said Jay.

"I don't know. The next clue to what?" said Lily. "We still don't actually know what we're looking for."

"Maybe we won't know until we've found it."

"But if we don't know what it is, how are we going to know that we've found it?"

Sam sat down heavily on the bench with a sigh. Her friends squeezed on either side of her. It was a bit tight but at least being crammed in made it a little warmer.

"I wish we had chips. Is it too early for chips?" said Jay.

"It's never too early for chips," said Sam.

"How can you possibly be hungry after the breakfast we just ate?" asked Lily.

Sam laughed. "Oh, so you've met Jay's mum? Did she ask when the two of you are getting married?"

Jay elbowed Sam. Lily grinned. "She did. I told her we were planning a June wedding."

"Brilliant. I'll buy a hat."

The sky was like spilled gold, running in thick rivulets towards the horizon. The houses and streets were washed in yellow and a slice of iron sea was visible, refusing to succumb to the brightness of the sunshine. Lily's happiness sat in her stomach, warming her from the inside out. It took her by surprise. She slid her arm through Sam's. Sam gave her a little squeeze.

"I've been following the guy from the photo," she said.

Lily nearly fell off the bench. "You've been doing *what now?*"

"I've been following him. Don't look at me like that. I wasn't exactly going to come tell you after you friend-dumped me."

Lily wriggled. Sam gave her arm another squeeze. "After the library, I was scared for a bit. And then I got really angry. And then, the more I thought about it, the more I thought you might be right. Not the us being boring and rubbish bit, but about the reading room being trashed because we were getting close enough to annoy someone. Or scare someone. And then I started thinking about that guy."

Lily chewed her bottom lip. "I have something to tell you. But you have to promise not to get angry with me."

Sam turned her whole body to look at Lily, almost knocking her off the bench again. "What is it?"

"I've met him."

This time, Sam did push Lily off the bench. Lily stood up, dusting herself off.

"What on earth do you mean, you've met him?"

"The guy in the photograph. He came up to me in the lanes one night and asked me about Emily. He knew we were looking for her. In fact, he seemed to think we'd already found her."

Sam shivered. "I wish. I should have let Costello savage him. Who is he? Why is he interested in Emily?"

"I doubt it's for the same reasons that we are. His name is Horace Snyde but I don't know who he is or how he knows Emily. What did you find out while you were following him?"

"Well, he's definitely a creep, that's for sure. I once saw him blow snot right out of his nose on to the street."

"Gross."

"Totally grim," agreed Sam. "Anyway. Beyond that, I haven't managed to learn all that much. He hangs around the library a lot."

"Doing research like us?"

Sam shook her head. "No, he doesn't go in. Just hangs around outside. He might be keeping an eye out for us, though, making sure we haven't started our investigations again."

"If he's looking for Emily, why would he be worried that we were getting close to finding something?" asked Jay. "Surely he'd want us to find her. So why trash the reading room?"

Lily shifted on her feet. "Maybe so we couldn't tell what he'd taken. I took a bunch of stuff home with me to keep working on, and there were definitely things missing. The photo of him. The notebook with all the stuff about Emily's mum."

"Do you think he knows about the museum?" said Jay.

Sam wrinkled her nose. "I hope not. He definitely hasn't been near it any time I've been following him."

"I haven't been back since ... since the reading room got trashed. I was afraid I'd lead him right to it," said Lily. "Maybe we'd better make sure Emily's things are still safe."

Eighteen

To their enormous relief, the museum looked exactly as it always had. Despite all the time that she had now spent here, it still took Lily's breath away. There was more than a touch of magic about the place, each tiny object transformed into a talisman, a clue. All three of them had spent untold hours staring in vain at buttons and books and flowers and hairbrushes, hoping that somehow they would reveal their secrets and slot some of the puzzle pieces into place.

They checked the whole museum. The first two rooms were small and oddly shaped, to fit into the fishermen's cottages, but once you got to the final room it opened up into what must have been a warehouse once upon a time. The room had been furnished in the same way as the others – beautiful dark wood, elegant lights, neat shelves. But the museum owner hadn't quite managed – or hadn't really wanted – to erase the history of the space. Every so often Lily would stumble upon a rotting barrel with a date burned into it, hundreds of years old. Or a crate with a fishing net thrown over it, frayed rope coiled up inside. The smell of alcohol and salt had been worn into the place and seemed to rise up from the very floorboards.

They were bickering about the significance of a few of the museum's exhibits when Lily heard the creak. She waved her arms at her friends, silencing them immediately. They stilled, ears pricked for any movement. There was nothing. Just the occasional sighing sound of the building settling around them.

"Maybe just the wind?" whispered Sam.

Lily's shoulders had relaxed just a fraction when the creak came again. Panic slammed into her stomach.

"There's someone else in here," hissed Lily.

She knew she wasn't the only one thinking of the trashed reading room – of the long, thin slices in their papers. Another creak, closer this time.

"We need to hide," said Lily. "Right now."

"Wait," said Sam. "What if it's him? We could confront him. If we surprise him, maybe he'll tell us what we need to know."

Lily widened her eyes at Sam. "I think I prefer terrified Sam to crazy Sam. What if he *was* trying to scare us off with the reading room? What do you think his next step would be?"

Another creak, closer again.

"Sam, Lily's right," said Jay. "We don't know what this guy is capable of. All we know is that the last kid to get involved with him disappeared without a trace."

"That's *terrifying*," said Lily. "What if he killed her and made this museum because he's still obsessed with her. Killers do that."

"That's right," said Jay. "They keep trophies."

"Would you two stop it? You're freaking me out."

"Maybe we *should* be freaking out."

"You're the one who wanted to be brave. A grand adventure! Whose idea was that?"

Creak... This time right at the top of the stairs. Lily grabbed her friends by the wrists and shoved them into a nearby crate. She clambered in on top of them, ignoring Sam's protests, and saw a shadow cross the doorway on the top level just as she tugged a pile of fishing net over the top of them.

Sam gagged slightly. "It smells horrendous in here."

Lily elbowed her in the ribs and put her finger emphatically to her lips. It did smell horrendous. Damp and fishy and who-knows-what-else. But remembering the sly, hungry look in Snyde's eyes as he asked her about Emily, she knew she'd rather be in here than out there facing him.

The iron stairs clanged gently as someone came down them. Lily had a mouthful of Sam's hair and was trying not to sneeze, and she was sure that her knee was jamming into Jay's side. They all held their breath, staying absolutely still and hoping that whoever it was would just go away. Lily tried to peer through the nets to see if she could see who it was and what they were doing, but it was no use. The thick ropes made everything grey and blurry. She took comfort in the fact that at least this probably meant whoever was out there couldn't see them either.

The footsteps drew agonisingly, terrifyingly close, the old floorboards murmuring a quiet warning to the hidden three. Then, silence. Lily's chest started to burn with the effort of holding her breath and she let it out slowly, as silently as she could. She shifted slightly, trying to see where the person had gone. The stairs hadn't made a noise, so she knew whoever it was hadn't gone away, but she couldn't hear them moving around any more.

Her back started to ache in the cramped space, and Sam's breath hot on her face made the crate seem even smaller and hotter than it really was. Her nose itched, tension was boiling in her stomach and the rotten, fishy smell seemed to be getting worse. With each second that passed, she became slightly more convinced that she'd rather take her chances with Snyde.

The quiet was becoming unbearable and Lily was seized with the crazy impulse to scream, just to break the silence and deal with whatever was going to happen. Sam was rigid beside her and Jay hardly seemed to be breathing at all.

Suddenly the fishing nets were ripped back. The three screamed, scrambling backwards away from their attacker, spilling out of the crate on to the museum floor.

Their screams mingled with a fourth. A distinctly feminine scream.

For a split second, Lily's panic was so enormous that neither the scream, nor the person it was coming from really registered. Her heart hammered in her chest and she struggled to get herself back under control. The other two seemed to be having the same fight. Jay had managed to get to his feet, his eyes darting wildly around, Sam was still half crouching, her hands balled in tight fists, her face clouding in confusion as the person in front of her came into focus.

"What are you doing here?"

Nineteen

"Ms Bright?" Lily asked. "Did you follow us?"

Ms Bright blinked at them in astonishment. "Did I... ? No, I didn't follow you. What are you three doing here? What is this place?"

Lily bit her lip and cast around for some kind of explanation. "We don't really know. How did you get here?"

"I ... I was invited," Ms Bright said.

Lily perked up. "Invited! Does that mean you know whose museum this is?"

Ms Bright shook her head and pulled a piece of paper from her pocket. A second sheet stuck to it, fluttering to the ground beside Lily. They crowded round to look at what Ms Bright was holding out to them. Lily blinked.

"It's a ticket!"

Curled and yellowed, but unmistakably a ticket.

The Museum of Emily: Grand Opening

All of your treasures but one

It was dated almost twenty years ago.

"Who gave this to you? Why would someone invite you here?" asked Sam.

Ms Bright shook her head, a strange look coming over her face. Lily stepped back slightly, her foot slipping on the paper that Ms Bright had dropped. She bent to pick it up and a cold fist squeezed her heart. It was the photograph of Snyde. She held it out

"Ms Bright, where did you get this photograph?"

Ms Bright turned pale, her eyes miserably downcast. Lily took another instinctive step backwards.

"It was you. You destroyed our reading room."

"I had to," said Ms Bright quietly.

Anger flushed through Lily, battling against her desire to run away.

"You had to? You scared the life out of us."

Ms Bright didn't say anything.

"Why? Why would you do something like that? I don't understand."

Ms Bright sighed. "I know. I know you don't understand. I don't understand either." She ran her hands agitatedly through her hair and held out the ticket to them. "I'm Emily."

Twenty

It was the middle of the night when Emily was shaken from her sleep. She had been having uneasy dreams and woke with a start, gasping for breath. As her eyes adjusted, she saw that Caitlyn was sitting on the side of her bed.

"Caitlyn? What's going on? What time is it?"

She reached for her bedside lamp, but Caitlyn grabbed her wrist before she could reach it.

"Don't! Leave it off."

The note of panic in her voice was high and sharp and it lodged between Emily's ribs like a thorn. She was suddenly wide awake. She sat up, shivering in the cold room. The fight between them was gone, washed away by whatever had frightened Caitlyn.

Caitlyn got up from the bed and started pulling open drawers. She yanked out Emily's clothes, dropping some on the floor and tossing others on to the bed.

"We'll take this, you like this one. And this. Where's that red jumper? It's warm. You didn't put it in the washing machine, did you?"

She moved to the wardrobe and started rummaging in there, stopping every so often to listen, although for what, Emily wasn't sure. Caitlyn pulled open a drawer with such ferocity that the corner dragged along her forearm, digging a tiny welt into her skin, which started to gleam red almost immediately. She didn't even notice. Emily pushed back her covers and ran to her sister.

"Caitlyn, stop. Stop. What is it? What's happened?"

Caitlyn sat on the edge of the drawers, sinking so that her face was level with Emily's. Her eyes were shining. She reached out and took Emily's face in both hands, smoothing her hair. Her face cracked in pain and Emily felt her heart jolt.

"I'm sorry. I tried to keep us safe but I can't."

Emily reached up and took one of Caitlyn's hands. "I don't understand. Keep us safe from what?"

Caitlyn squeezed her eyes shut and a single fat tear dropped down her face.

Emily felt her throat close. "The man. The one you wouldn't talk about."

Caitlyn kept her eyes closed and slumped forward, shaking her head violently. Emily grabbed her by the shoulders.

"Who is he? What has he done?"

Caitlyn sniffed. She swiped the tear from her face and straightened up slowly, as though she was gathering her strength. A few seconds later she was still pale and shaken but looked calmer. Determined. Emily straightened herself too, borrowing bravado from her sister.

"He's our cousin, sort of."

"Our *cousin*?"

Emily was astonished. She had always looked at enormous, sprawling families with jealousy. As far as she had known, she, Caitlyn and their mother had been the only members of their family left.

"Well, maybe more like mum's third cousin. I don't know. Related, but from generations ago."

"And why is he here? What does he want?"

Caitlyn laughed, just a single burst at first, but then it grew, multiplying until her eyes bulged wide and her whole body was shaking. Emily was frightened.

She wasn't sure what she'd do if Caitlyn had lost her mind.

"Caitlyn, stop it. Tell me what he wants."

The laughter cut off as suddenly as it had begun. Caitlyn shook her head and coolly met Emily's eye.

"He thinks we have the diamond."

Emily was baffled. "What diamond?"

"The diamond. The family diamond."

Suddenly Emily understood the laughter. "The diamond isn't real."

"I know. I've tried to tell him that. Believe me, I've tried."

"Does he think that if we had a diamond the size of a man's fist, we'd be living in an old fishing cottage in Edge?"

"*I know*. I know. I have no idea why he thinks it's real. But he does. He really does. I think—"

Caitlyn swallowed her words. She took a deep, steadying breath and tried again. "I think he killed Mum."

Emily reeled. Tears sprang to her eyes and spilled over, her head spinning wildly. Rage rose in the back of her throat and spread thickly over her tongue.

"He killed our mum over a bedtime story?"

"I know. It's ridiculous." Caitlyn laughed again, tugging hard at her own hair. "I don't understand it either."

When she spoke again, Emily's voice was small. "Is he going to kill us?"

Caitlyn nibbled at her thumbnail, tearing the tender skin around the nail bed. She shook her head. "I don't think so. But he said that if we didn't give him the diamond, he'd take you away from me."

Emily grabbed Caitlyn's hand, aware that she was digging her nails in too hard but unable to stop. "You mean he wants to kidnap me?"

"No, not kidnap you. It wouldn't be as hard as that. He said that if we didn't tell him where it was, he'd go to the police and tell them I couldn't look after you properly."

"That's crazy. No one could look after me better than you. They wouldn't believe him."

Caitlyn's face was strained. "They would. You said it yourself. I'm a kid looking after another kid."

Emily felt sick.

"He's been watching us ever since Mum disappeared. I know he's getting ready to make his move. We need to leave. You and me. Tonight."

Emily swallowed hard. "Where will we go?"

"Don't worry. I'm going to take care of you. But we need to get ready right now. One bag; only take what you absolutely need."

Caitlyn kissed Emily's head, pressing her lips hard into the crown of her hair. She stroked her cheek and went back to her room, leaving Emily to deal with what she had just heard. Almost on autopilot, Emily started to pick things up and lay them out on the bed. Her favourite things. Her treasures, as she had come to think of them. It quickly became clear that she wasn't going to be able to carry them all. Tears pricked again at the back of her eyes and she burned all over with the injustice of it.

She pulled her rucksack from under the bed and started to pack sensibly. Warm clothes; a few books. She pulled photographs from frames and tucked them into the pages. Her mum's apple pie recipe still lay on her desk from her birthday. She tucked it into her pocket and then pulled it out again. She already knew it by heart.

She packed her treasures into boxes, laying the apple pie recipe on top. Trinkets, objects scavenged from the beach, little reminders of who she was, who she had been and who she hoped to be.

She prised up the loose boards of her floor. There was a huge space under there, big enough that she sometimes used to climb in and lie in there when she was feeling overwhelmed. She was suddenly seized with the urge to do that now. Bring Caitlyn in and hide them both safely in the dark. She pushed her boxes into the space and replaced the floorboards.

Finally she picked up her favourite book, her library card stuck inside to mark her place. She opened her backpack to put it in and then stopped. Instead, she lifted the floorboards and slid it into the top box. A sort of promise to herself. She laid her hand flat on the floor.

"I'll come back. Someday, I'll come back. When it's safe."

Twenty-One

Lily sat in Ms Bright's kitchen with Sam and Jay, a cup of tea cooling between her fingers, watching as the sycamore tree outside dropped its leaves like little yellow stars. As she finished her story, Ms Bright – Emily – tilted her head upwards, as though to hold the tears that had gathered in her eyes.

A million questions tumbled in Lily's mind, stacking up, tripping over each other and getting stuck. A glance at her friends told her that they were feeling the same way. The silence stretched, filled with all the things no one knew how to say. For a while, the ticking of the clock on the wall was the only sound.

Lily lifted her cold cup to her lips, sipped, winced. "I'm so sorry, Ms Bright."

It sounded insignificant but it was all that could be said. Ms Bright blinked her tears away and straightened her shirt.

"It was a long time ago."

"What happened to Caitlyn?" asked Lily.

"She's OK. We lost everything else but we got to

keep each other. We even stayed Caitlyn and Emily McCrae for a while. And then we started to see this man popping up everywhere we went. Asking questions. It wasn't safe to be us any more. We had to become different people."

"You became Ms Bright."

Ms Bright smiled. "Bright was Caitlyn's idea. Our family once owned the old town lighthouse, you know. So we picked a name that let us keep some of our old selves close to our hearts. She was too frightened to come back when I did, even after nearly twenty years. I guess she was right."

"What made you come back to Edge?" said Sam.

Ms Bright was quiet for a moment, then said simply, "This is my home."

Lily tapped the ticket lying on the table. "So where does the museum come into it?"

Ms Bright shook her head. "I have absolutely no idea. I didn't know anything about the museum until today."

"Did someone send the ticket to you?"

"No. I found it under the floorboards of my old

house. I never went back, you see. Thought it was too risky. But then after the reading room—" Her head jerked slightly but she pressed on. "After the reading room, I realised you had seen the things I had hidden. At first I thought I was being paranoid, but there were things in your notes that you couldn't possibly have known. So I went back to look."

"And?"

"And they were gone. The only thing in there was the ticket, and it was so dusty that I almost didn't see it."

"So the exhibits in the museum...?"

"Everything in that museum is something that I hid when we ran away. Everything except this."

Ms Bright placed an object in the middle of the table. The "X marks the spot" note.

"The secret!" exclaimed Lily.

"It *is* a treasure hunt," said Jay. "Just like your ticket said! 'All of your treasures but one.' Someone is laying out a treasure hunt for you."

"A treasure hunt for what?" said Ms Bright.

Lily blinked at her. "For the diamond."

Ms Bright shook her head. "There is no diamond. There was never a diamond. It's just an old story."

"What makes you so sure?" said Lily.

Ms Bright fixed her with that infuriatingly familiar look that all adults give children just before they say "You're too young to understand". Before she could speak, Sam butted in.

"It's not as outlandish as it sounds."

"Good use of 'outlandish'," said Jay.

"Thanks. We know that the town had pirates. We've all seen the caves and the tunnels and the old warehouses like your museum, Ms Bright. That's not fantasy. That's history."

"Once you eliminate the impossible, whatever remains – however improbable – must be the truth. Sherlock Holmes said that," said Jay.

"I shouldn't have given you all those books. They've burrowed too deep into your brain."

"That's exactly why you *should* have given us all the books, and you know it. If we weren't on the lookout for a mystery, Lily would never have found your museum."

"How *did* you find the museum, Lily?"

"I'm not sure. I just sort of ... did."

Sam turned triumphantly. "You see? Doesn't that sound like magic to you? Lily finds the museum and brings it to me. I bring her to you. We give up and the museum brings you back to us."

"In a town this small, I don't think that's as improbable as you think it is. Just because you want to believe something doesn't make it true."

"And just because you *don't* want to doesn't make it *not* true. It's real, Ms Bright. We've been following the clues—"

"Stop. It sounds more like a trap than a treasure hunt. I don't want the three of you involved in this."

"You're seriously telling me that there's a whole secret museum dedicated to you and you're not the least bit curious why?"

"Of course I'm curious. But this isn't a fun storybook adventure. *He's* here. People could get hurt. People *have* been hurt. I want you to promise me that you won't go digging around any more."

"But, Ms Bright—"

"No! I will take care of this. Promise you won't put yourselves in harm's way."

Lily sighed heavily. "We promise."

She felt a little guilty for lying but sometimes grown-ups were just too grown-up to understand.

The three returned to the bench, this time – at Sam's insistence – with a bag of chips. They sat very quietly for a while, absorbing what Ms Bright had told them.

Lily couldn't believe that Ms Bright was willing to believe that her distant cousin had murdered her mother for no reason but couldn't entertain the idea that a pirate might have given her great-great-grandpa a diamond. Adults were baffling sometimes.

"We're not giving up, right?" said Jay.

"Absolutely not," said Sam and Lily in unison. They grinned at each other.

"So what now? We can't use the library any more, now that she knows what we've been working on."

Lily shook her head. "Isn't it weird, that it was Ms Bright the whole time? No wonder Snyde thought we'd found her."

"Explains why he's been casing the library too. Just waiting for the right moment to do something awful."

"So why hasn't he made his move? He's been here for weeks."

"The town is small. One good scream and he'd be toast. The McCraes lived right out on the edge of the sea but Ms Bright lives in town."

"And we know he's patient. He's waited twenty years. He can afford to wait for the perfect opportunity."

This did not make Lily feel better. She wriggled. "I feel like we've been poking around in her head."

"I know what you mean," said Sam. "It's weird to think that an adult could have stolen lipsticks from her sister and written notes in class and kept a pencil just because a boy loaned it to her. Just like any of us. Even though I obviously knew Emily was alive years and years ago, I was still picturing a girl like me."

"Ms Bright is a girl like you."

"She is not! No way I'd have grown up with a family legend about a diamond and not gone digging around for it."

Lily looked up. "Maybe she did."

"She already said she doesn't believe in it."

"Yeah, she doesn't. But that doesn't mean that she never did. You're right, it would be mad to grow up with a legend like that and not go looking for it. I would have done."

"So would I," said Jay.

"So maybe she did. And maybe she got closer than she realised."

"Right. Or her mum did. Or her sister."

"And that's why Snyde came after them."

"What do we do? Ms Bright is right, Snyde is dangerous. Maybe we need some help," said Lily.

"What kind of help?"

"I don't know. Maybe we should go to the police. If we tell them that there's someone dangerous in town, they'd have to help us."

"No way," said Sam. "Even Ms Bright doesn't believe us. There's no chance the police would."

"So what do we do?" asked Jay.

Lily blew a curl out of her face. "I have absolutely no idea."

Twenty-Two

Every year on the first of December, for reasons that were totally unfathomable to Lily, Edge threw a beach party. As the sky cracked with frost and the air grew so cold that Lily could constantly see her breath in front of her face, the people of Edge took to the sands.

Bonfires dotted the seaside, throwing wild, dancing shadows around and filling the night with the tang of burning wood. People huddled around them, wrapped in ten layers, cradling mugs of steaming spiced rum. Someone had set up a hot dog stand and someone else was selling ice creams.

Lily stood on the beachfront with her friends, writing her name in the air with a fizzing sparkler. She was wearing so many jumpers under her coat that she could hardly bend her arms, and a hat with an enormous pompom bobbed cheerily above her face, occasionally falling over her eyes and blinding her completely.

Cold and laughter were making her giddy, although

not as giddy as her mum, who had been sipping from a silver flask brought by Jay's mum and was now leaning against her, laughing hysterically.

Sam had procured a toffee apple from somewhere and was using it as a baton to guide the adults in a rowdy chorus of a Christmas song, snapping photographs in every direction.

Cold nibbled at Lily's nose, pinching her cheeks to a vivid red. She bought a hot chocolate from one of the vans on the promenade and held it tight, the warmth seeping through her gloves to her stiff fingers. Jay appeared beside her, an enormous scarf wrapped all the way round his face.

"My mum is drunk!" he said, his voice disappearing into the sea of knitwear he was wearing. "She says your mum is a bad influence."

"Hey, my mum is not the one who brought a flask."

"They're having loads of fun. Maybe we should go and send them to their rooms."

"Let's."

Jay raised his paper cup. "Cheers."

They clinked cups. They heard the click of Sam's

camera and turned. She had two enormous woolly blankets slung over her shoulder. They were almost as big as she was.

"Come here, Lily. I want to show you something," she said.

They picked their way across the beach, until the clamour of misbehaving grown-ups and the light of the bonfires faded behind them. Sam spread one blanket on the ground. She gestured to her friends.

"Lie down."

"Have you lost it?" said Lily.

Sam rolled her eyes. "I remember when you didn't talk so much. Would you just lie down?"

Lily did. As Sam and Jay got on either side of her, she gasped. Away from the light of the fires and the promenade, the sky was more stars than darkness. Sam pulled the second blanket over them but Lily had already forgotten how cold she was. As her eyes adjusted, more and more stars came into view, peppering the inky sky.

"There's Orion's Belt, see?"

Sam was pointing to the three diagonal stars to

their left. Lily had seen Orion's Belt before: it was one of the few constellations bright enough to see even in the city, but the surrounding fuzz of new stars had made it unfamiliar now.

"And the Plough." Sam pointed again.

The white band of the Milky Way stretched above their heads and Lily finally understood what people meant when they said that something had taken their breath away. She started to feel dizzy. She twined her fingers into Sam's on one side and Jay's on the other. They were squeezed in tight, huddled together for warmth.

"I'm going to remember this for my whole life. Forever."

No one replied. No one had to. A shooting star streaked past and something inside Lily leapt. She made a wish, her face flushing at its cheesiness. She was glad it was too dark for the others to see her blush. She wondered if they were wishing the same thing. Forever.

A scream jolted Lily from her reverie. She bolted upright, eyes darting around.

"What was that?"

Further screams tore from down the beach. Jay and Sam burst out laughing.

"Oh no."

"What is it? What's going on?"

"Total madness, that's what's going on. Come and see."

They picked their way back down the beach. As they came back into the crowds, Lily's mouth dropped open again. People were tugging off their layers and plunging laughingly into the freezing sea.

"What on...?"

Sam clutched her sides. "It's the December dip! Honestly, I don't even know how to explain. Maybe you were right about Edge to begin with. Everyone is bananas."

"Why would anyone want to go in the water?"

Jay shrugged. "Tradition?"

"Tradition is a terrible reason to do anything. Elephants in circuses was tradition. And women not having the vote."

"You're probably right. Want to go in?"

"Definitely not."

Sam elbowed her. "Ah, come on. We'll just dip our toes. It'll make you a real Edger."

"One: an Edger is not a thing. Two: I am definitely not an Edger."

She turned to Jay for support but he had already sat down to untie his shoes. She followed them to the water's edge, shoes still stubbornly on her feet. Sam screeched as the water washed over her toes. She hopped from foot to foot, her squeals turning to hysterical laughter. She threw her head back and mockingly howled at the moon.

"This town is so weird," said Lily, shaking her head and bending to pull off her boots.

As the first wave washed over her feet, Lily genuinely worried that she might be having a heart attack. Needles of cold pushed into every inch of her exposed skin, filling her with a burning, frenzied pain. Her breath caught in her throat, wheezing uselessly out of her. Her chest ached. She turned furiously to her friends but as she did, the adrenalin hit her heart like a punch. Her skin sang with it, her mind focused to a pinprick, colours burned so bright that she had to turn away from the bonfires.

She screamed, the pain and her laughter escaping in one go, and jumped up and down in the water, relishing the snap of cold water rising over her ankles. She looked at the people who were fully submerged, splashing in the water. No way. That was a step too far. She wriggled her toes under the water's surface, feeling shells and sand crackle under her. Ripples rose around her, blurring the reflected moonlight, slicing it into thin shards and sending it out across the water.

Sam nudged her gently. "Come on, we'd better get out. You shouldn't stay in for more than a few minutes. Half the town will be down with a cold tomorrow."

Grudgingly, Lily followed them back out of the water towards the bonfire. Sam's dad had brought about fifteen spare pairs of woollen socks, all of which he had made himself. Lily accepted them gratefully, rolling them over her frozen toes.

She stuck her feet by the bonfire, ignoring Sam's warnings not to and was immediately taken down by a debilitating case of pins and needles as the blood rushed back. She howled. Sam shrugged smugly. Lily wiggled her toes, her cold joints cracking. She drew her feet in and rubbed them vigorously between her palms. She felt like she was rubbing her skin off but gradually the prickling sensation started to die down. More screams rose from the water's edge and Lily turned to look. "You people are not normal, you know. Why would anyone do something that hurts that much?"

Sam laughed. "Someone's got into the water too fast."

"Or got out and just remembered it's December."

"Or stuck their feet by the bonfire even though they were told not to." Sam's grin fell from her face as the screams grew and multiplied. "Wait. Something's wrong."

They ran towards the sound, Lily wincing every time her feet hit the sand. A group of adults were standing shivering on the beach, their faces pale, hands clamped over their mouths. They were crowded around something huddled and soaking on the sand.

It was a person, a glistening rope of blood winding its way down their face, their lips blue and unmoving.

As she made out the face of the figure in the sand, Lily let out a gasp of horror.

"It's Ms Bright."

Twenty-Three

They weren't allowed to see Ms Bright. She had been rushed to hospital and was barely conscious; definitely not up for visitors. She had suffered concussion from the bang on her head, but it was the cold water that had almost killed her. If someone hadn't spotted her and pulled her out, she would have been dead within a few minutes. It had been chalked up as an accident, a slip on some rocks, an accidental bump from an overexcited swimmer. But Lily felt as though a shadow had fallen over the town, drawing ever closer to her and her friends.

They went to check on the museum, superstitiously frightened that something might have happened to it. Lily shivered as she walked down the now familiar lane, remembering Ms Bright's frozen face, her glassy eyes. Lily had thought she was dead. They all had.

"Do you think it was him?" asked Sam. "Do you think he tried to kill her?"

Lily tugged at her hair. "I don't know. What would that get him?"

"Maybe he was threatening her and went too far?"

"Maybe. It was the perfect opportunity. No one would have noticed anything. Not in all the chaos of the dip. How long was that person screaming before anyone realised something was wrong?" Lily balled her fists into her eyes as she shouldered the museum's green door open and made her way up the spiral steps. "I don't like this."

"Me neither," said Sam.

She walked into the back of Lily, who had stopped abruptly at the entrance to the museum's first room. She peered around her.

"Oh."

The exhibits gleamed under sparkling glass cabinets. The yellow light from the bulbs overhead reflected gently off the polished wooden floorboards. Every speck of dirt was gone.

"Ms Bright," said Lily.

"It must have been," said Jay. "Maybe she couldn't stand to see her treasures like that."

The objects almost seemed to glow in their cases, technicolour without the layer of dust Lily had got used to seeing them under. The museum looked more beautiful than ever. Sam grasped for Lily's hand.

"Look." She pointed. "The apple pie recipe is gone."

They approached the empty case. In the wood where the frame had been, someone had scratched three words. A tiny rebellion in the immaculate room. *Emily was here.* They stood staring at it for a long time.

"She was going to run," said Sam. "And she took her mum's recipe. She wasn't planning to come back."

Lily's face was hot. "It's not fair. She was going to lose everything all over again. We have to help her."

"Maybe you were right before," said Sam. "Maybe we should go to the police."

"I think maybe we have to. Ms Bright could have died. I don't think this is a job for a bunch of twelve-year-olds."

The police station was an ugly concrete cube in the centre of town. It looked as though it had been specifically designed to be hideous. Lily shifted nervously as they passed through the door. She felt as though she was doing something wrong just by being there. The man who met them seemed familiar in a way that Lily couldn't quite place until he said his name.

"Sergeant Bruce," he said, emphasis firmly placed on the first word, as though to highlight that it should be treated with appropriate respect.

Lily remembered the built-up chair in the headmistress's office and had to bite the inside of her mouth to keep from laughing. She felt Sam beside her, struggling not to look at her. She kept her eyes firmly fixed on the police officer, freezing her chest and taking deep, calming breaths.

He led them through fluorescently lit corridors and into a grim little room. It looked dark, even though it wasn't, as though it had deliberately been decorated to look grimy. Sad chairs lined a table and he steered the three into them. He sat opposite, scratching his nose with the tip of his pencil.

"So you're here about Ms Bright's accident."

"Yes, sir," said Lily. She arranged her face into its most solemn and trustworthy expression. "We're not so sure it was an accident."

Sergeant Bruce grunted, still picking at his nose with the pencil. Sam had adopted the same angelic expression as Lily. It looked wrong on her face.

"We think that someone deliberately hurt Ms Bright because they believe her to be in possession of a diamond that once belonged to a pirate and they would like to steal it. Sir."

She spoke with as much gravitas as she could muster, hoping some of it might rub off on the police officer.

His wide, watery mouth stretched in displeasure. "I don't think it's very good of you to come in here and make a joke about poor Ms Bright. Her accident was extremely serious, you know. She was very lucky not to have died."

"We know that it's serious," said Lily, struggling to control the volume of her voice. "That's why we've come to the police station."

Sergeant Bruce fixed her with a grave look. "So Ms Bright – the librarian – has a diamond."

"Well, *we* don't think she has it. But he does."

"OK. And who is *he*?"

"We think he's a relative of hers. His name is Horace Snyde."

"Let me clarify. You think that a relative of Ms Bright's, who you don't really know, might have tried to murder her because he thinks that she might have a diamond that was given to her by a pirate, but that you don't think she really has it."

"That's right," said Lily. "More or less. Don't you want to write any of this down?"

"No, Millie, I don't."

"It's Lily."

"Do you and your friends understand that wasting police time could get you into a lot of trouble?"

"We're not—"

"Do you know that we're doing lots of very important work keeping this town safe, and you are taking time away from that?"

"Yes, but—"

"Now, I'd hate to have to involve your parents in this. I suggest you take your little story out of here and let us get on with solving real crimes."

He grimaced as they yelled their response, talking over each other and waving their arms impassionedly, and then, as soon as they had quietened down, he led them out of the station.

Sam stared at the door of the station as it swung closed behind them, her mouth agape.

"Can you believe him?"

"I know. And Sergeant Bruce..."

"They've got to be related."

"A brother, maybe. Surely no one would marry either of them."

"We should have sent Jay on his own. Adults always like him better than me."

"I wonder why." Lily reached out and tugged a leaf from Sam's long hair.

"Whatever. Being a mess is part of my charm. Not my fault that the grown-ups don't see it."

"I know. So, the police don't want to help."

"And Ms Bright can't help."

"Oh, man. I was really hoping this wouldn't be a job for a bunch of twelve-year-olds."

Twenty-Four

Snyde seemed to have disappeared.

Lily suspected he had gone to ground after attacking Ms Bright, waiting to snatch her again when she got out of hospital. She hoped that when Ms Bright woke up she'd go to the police. But she'd been so frightened, Lily thought she'd probably just run. So she, Sam and Jay decided to track down Snyde's hideout themselves.

Lily was dressed in black, even though they were going out in the daytime. She wasn't sure what would camouflage her in daylight, but hoped that black would at least make her nondescript. Jay had obviously had the same thought and was also wearing black from head to toe. Sam hadn't quite followed suit, sporting her traditional tartan coat and an enormous red headband.

They brought Costello, hoping his tracking instincts might kick in and lead them straight to Snyde.

They passed the bench with its stupid, meaningless dedication. Lily glared at it. Just a boring bench, surrounded by other boring benches with more boring dedications. She bent to read the one next to it.

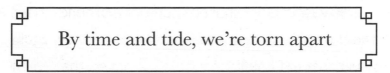

By time and tide, we're torn apart

Lily rolled her eyes. Whoever wrote that one had obviously been feeling a bit maudlin. And everyone in this town was obsessed with the sea. She gave the bench a kick and continued on her way. They wandered around Edge aimlessly for about half an hour before striking gold.

"Bingo!" whispered Sam, pointing to a nearby gutter.

"Why are you whispering?"

"For dramatic effect. Look, this is perfect."

She was pointing to a cigarette butt, tossed on to a drain cover.

"Every time we've seen him he's been surrounded by a cloud of smoke. I bet this is his."

"We don't know that. Costello could end up leading us to some poor unfortunate person who just happens to be a smoker."

"But this has been thrown in the street. That's exactly the sort of villainous thing he would do."

Sam wrapped her scarf round her hand and pinched the cigarette butt carefully between her fingers. She held it out to Costello.

"Here you go, boy. Find! Seek!"

Costello sneezed. Sam frowned. "Come on, Costello. This is your moment. Find him! Track him down!"

Costello put his face obediently to the cigarette butt. He gave it an experimental lick. Sam jerked it away from him and stuffed it into her pocket.

"What kind of a sniffer dog are you?"

He looked up at them with doleful eyes. Sam rolled her eyes and scratched behind his ear. "You really are the most ridiculous dog."

Costello shook himself and then sat bolt upright, ears moving, nose twitching. He whined slightly and then dashed forward, jerking impatiently at his lead.

"Sam, he's doing it! He's taking us to him!"

"We have to be careful. This is strictly a reconnaissance mission."

"You watch too much TV."

"Whatever. Let's go!"

Costello led them confidently through the streets, stopping every so often to stick his nose in the air and confirm that they were heading in the right direction. They picked up the pace, jogging behind him, struggling to keep up with his excited pulling. Lily's heart was beating in her ears. They twisted through the town, white houses passing in a blur, dodging round other people, pushing through little crowds, yelling their apologies behind them as they ran.

And finally they burst out of an alleyway on to the sandy beach, where Costello proceeded to start digging an enthusiastic hole, looking thrilled with himself.

"The beach?!" yelled Sam. "You've brought us to the beach?! You useless, self-centred, nonsense dog, I'll have you made into a rug."

"You know he doesn't understand you, right?"

Costello barked contentedly, grinning a huge slobbery grin.

"Wipe that smile off your face right now. We are trying to solve a mystery and you're dragging us to the beach? What are you bringing to the table if you can't even track a villain?"

"He still can't understand you."

"Don't be daft. He understands every word I say. He's the only one that listens to me half the time."

"Sam—"

"No, it's true. I know that I talk too much. It's fair enough that everyone else gets bored—"

"Sam—"

"But he's such a good listener—"

Lily clamped one hand over Sam's mouth and pointed down the length of the beach with the other. In the distance, standing at the shoreline, was a familiar slouching figure. Sam's eyes widened.

"Costello, you genius. The greatest, smartest dog in the whole world. I knew you could do it."

Costello woofed a smug reply, shaking himself happily.

"Go get him!" said Sam, unhooking Costello's collar from his lead.

Costello hared off in entirely the wrong direction, barking at a disgruntled flock of seagulls. Sam planted her hands on her hips, her brow creasing in a frown.

"That's probably for the best," said Jay. "I thought this was strictly a reconnaissance mission."

Sam blushed. "True. I got excited."

In the distance, Snyde turned away from the sea and started to walk.

"Come on, let's see where he goes."

They crept along the beach, leaving Costello to his seagulls. The sand was not an easy surface to be sneaky on, but they did their best, lifting their feet gently to mask the wet, sucking sounds, and keeping low to the ground, ducking behind rocks and enormous pieces of driftwood. Eventually they drew close enough to confirm that the man was definitely Snyde.

He turned towards them and Lily dragged Sam and Jay behind a crop of dark rocks, her back pressing against the rough surface, her heart hammering in her chest. They were close enough that they could hear the decisive strike of his match, the sizzle as he tossed it into a rock pool. Lily wrinkled her nose. She hated him.

After a minute or so she cautiously peeked over the top of the rock and then stood up straight, looking all around in bafflement.

"What is it?" whispered Jay.

"He's gone!" said Lily.

Jay stood, put a hand up to shield his eyes and scanned the beach. Lily was right. Snyde had gone. His footprints were still just visible in the sand, flooded and half washed away by the encroaching tide.

"I don't understand. He was right there," said Lily.

Jay walked to where his footprints were being erased and looked along the water's edge.

"How can someone just disappear into thin air?" said Lily.

Jay turned to her triumphantly. "Not into thin air. Into solid rock."

He pointed. Lily and Sam followed his gaze and gasped. Of course. This was pirate country. The face of the cliff was riddled with caves.

Twenty-Five

Lily, Sam and Jay padded across the wet sand to where Snyde had disappeared. Costello whined after them from the promenade, where Sam had looped his lead round a lamppost. Lily shivered as they approached the mouth of the nearest cave. She had never noticed how apt the word "mouth" was before. It yawned in front of them, huge and dark, ridged with pointed rocks. As they stepped inside Lily was seized with the fear that it would slam shut behind them, swallowing them whole.

It was even colder inside the cave. Damp air settled on Lily's hair and skin, beading into freezing droplets that ran down her neck. The floor was slick with seaweed and Sam grabbed for Lily's arm as she slipped. Their footsteps splashed softly, echoing around the space.

Lily clicked on her torch. The cave was enormous, much bigger than it looked from the outside. The thin light from the torch only seemed to emphasise how dark it was. She darted the beam around, expecting something terrible to loom out from the shadows at any moment. The shush of the waves, the lapping water, made Lily feel uneasy. It sounded as though something was rising from the sea, something that was getting ready to snatch at her ankles.

They made their way further into the cave and for a while Lily was glad to leave the sloshing sound of the waves behind. But the silence was worse; much worse. Their scuffling footsteps echoed and multiplied around them. Huge droplets of water fell from the cave ceiling high above, plinking loudly to the wet ground. Every so often something would skitter past them. Lily tried not to look, afraid it would be a rat or a giant spider.

The daylight behind them shrank to a pinprick as they turned a corner. Disgust curled in Lily's stomach as she patted the slimy walls of the cave, searching for anything hidden in its alcoves. Twice she lost her footing, once stepping heavily into a hidden pool. Terror seized her as the ground disappeared from underneath her, but the pool was only a few inches deep and her foot collided heavily with its uneven bottom. There was a sickening crunch and she sucked in a long breath through her teeth. For a second she was sure she must have broken her ankle but, gingerly testing it out, she could still put weight on it. Thank goodness. She had no idea how she'd explain a broken ankle to her mum, given that she'd told her she was only going to Jay's house to study. Her foot twinged with pain and cold, her shoe sloshing out water with every step.

Her torch beam suddenly picked out a horrifying, pale figure. She recoiled, crying out. It was a dead seagull, washed into the cave, half buried in seaweed. She stepped backwards and yelled out again as her dry foot slid into another pool. She spun, angrily pointing her torch, and bumped into Sam, standing frozen with terror.

She hadn't stepped in another pool. The sea had caught up to them. She had been so focused on moving forward that she hadn't stopped to look behind her, hadn't noticed the water rising, creeping ever closer.

"Sam," Lily croaked.

Sam couldn't answer, her eyes darting around the cave floor as though she couldn't understand where it had gone.

"Oh, no," said Jay. "These caves fill up when the tide comes in. We need to get out of here right now."

"Maybe there's a way through," said Lily. She wished her voice didn't sound so pathetic. "Lots of the caves lead out to the town."

"No way, we can't take that chance. What if we hit a dead end? Look how fast the water has risen."

Nausea swept through Lily. She took a few deep, gulping breaths, the taste of salt and mould and seaweed hitting her hard in the back of the throat. She reached out her foot tentatively, stretching it along the cave floor. The water rose over her ankle.

"It's not too deep yet. We can get back to the shore."

"We can't see the floor. We have no idea how deep it is."

"We don't have any other choice. We need to go. Now."

She turned and headed towards the hidden

entrance of the cave, her insides churning, her feet cramping in the freezing water. She focused on the splashing footsteps of her friends behind her, concentrating hard on leading them to safety, forcing herself to keep putting one foot in front of the other.

The water was up to her knees now. It slowed her down, dragging her back as it flowed towards the darkness in the throat of the cave. She reached a hand behind her. Sam clasped it and stretched out her own hand to Jay. They held each other tight, pulling forward as one. The breath burst from Lily as they rounded the corner and saw the mouth of the cave ahead of them, tantalisingly close.

The sea was rushing in faster, white froth smashing furiously into the sides. Every step seemed to take forever, Lily's heavy winter clothes filling with water and weighing her down. It was like being in a nightmare, where she knew something terrible was chasing her but couldn't seem to move her feet. She pressed on and suddenly the ground disappeared under her feet.

She sank up to her waist, all the breath knocked

out of her. She was paralysed by the pain, like a thousand needles jamming into her. Sam stood on the ledge Lily had just stepped off, her face a mask of fear, still clutching Lily's hand. Lily clenched her teeth so hard she was afraid she'd crack them, and tugged at Sam.

"Come on. You have to keep coming."

Sam nodded, her mouth set in a grim line of determination. Her fingers tightened round Lily's and she closed her eyes as she stepped off the ledge. She couldn't stop the scream escaping her lips. Jay followed, bending double as the cold hit him like a punch in the gut. The three were shaking uncontrollably now.

Lily tried not to think of all the things she'd heard people say about Ms Bright's accident. *She was lucky that she'd been spotted. Just a few minutes in that water could have killed her. Just a few minutes.* The beach was almost within reach. Just a few more steps. Just a few more.

The water surged again, closing over her stomach. Her hand hit the jagged mouth of the cave, just as

Sam tripped behind her and disappeared into the water.

"Sam!" she yelled.

Ignoring the pain, she plunged downwards after her friend, yanking her back upright. Water crashed violently into the cave, tugging them both backwards. Lily braced herself against the onslaught and clung to the rocks. Sam shook her head, her eyes wild and red.

"I can't. I'm too tired. I need to rest."

Lily put her hands on Sam's shoulders, rubbing her to keep her warm. "Yes you can. Look at me. Sam, look at me." Sam lifted bleary eyes to Lily's face. "You can do this. I know you can. Come on. Let's get somewhere safe."

She laced her fingers into Sam's but they were hit by another wave, tearing them apart. Lily clutched at the rock face, its barnacled surface scraping her hands raw. She struggled, salt burning the back of her throat. Panic washed over her in huge waves. She couldn't see Sam or Jay any more.

With an almighty heave, she pulled herself round

the mouth of the cave. The sea continued to rush towards her, pinning her against the cliff. She scrabbled for purchase against the sandy sea floor and waded through the breakers, dropping heavily on to the sand. She felt dizzy with relief as she saw Jay struggling towards her, Sam's arm draped round his shoulders. She splashed towards them, pulling them both to the safety of the beach, where they lay exhausted in the shallows. Sam coughed up a mouthful of seawater. Her lips were tinged with blue, her teeth chattering heavily. Lily herself probably didn't look any better. Her eyes filled. She shook her head at Jay.

"We could have died," he said in a tiny voice.

Lily didn't know how to reply. Sam still wasn't talking. It was probably the longest Lily had ever heard her go without speaking. She had no idea what she was going to tell her mum.

Twenty-Six

When Lily arrived home soaked and shivering, her mum screamed. Lily opened her mouth to explain but suddenly found that she was too tired to make her lips move. Her mind grew slow and foggy as she fell against something warm and soft. She could see goosebumps rising on her mum's skin as drops of water fell on it from her own hair. She buried her face in the crook of her mum's neck, dimly aware that her mum's skin felt scalding against hers. She frowned. Was her mum sick? That didn't seem right, but Lily couldn't quite put her finger on why. If she could just sleep for a while, she would remember.

She was stripped of her wet clothes and tucked into bed under three layers of blankets. Her mum held a cup of tea to her lips, pouring small sips into her mouth. Her face was pale and old-looking. She was shaking her head and saying something. Lily thought she might be in trouble but the words floated around, bouncing off her gently. She pulled the blankets up to her chin and closed her eyes. After a while, her mum's footsteps receded and the bedroom door clicked behind her.

The next morning Lily awoke, feeling unbelievably sick, to the news that she and her friends had all been grounded and forbidden from seeing each other.

"You're banning me from my friends?"

Lily's mum placed a cup of tea in front of her daughter. "Don't be so dramatic. Nobody is banning anything. We just think it's a good idea to let you have a little bit of space from each other."

"I don't need space. I don't *want* space. My friends are the only good thing about this stupid town you made me move to."

Her mum flinched but held her ground. Lily had used that particular guilt trip often since being told that they were leaving the city and now, just when she needed it most, it had worn thin.

Without her friends, Edge felt as cold and empty as it had when Lily first arrived. Her mum was trying to make up for it, being overly cheery and constantly present until Lily wanted to scream at her to go away. Her phone had been confiscated, so she couldn't even send a message to see how Sam and Jay were getting on. Ms Bruce was only too happy to enforce the ban at school, patrolling the lunch hall to make sure they were staying apart. Lily was suddenly, desperately lonely.

She had thought about writing notes on paper aeroplanes and tossing them at Sam's house from her bedroom window, but it turned out that seaside winters were quite a different animal to city winters. The wind was violent and unpredictable, literally sweeping Lily off her feet occasionally and battering the town with spray, no matter how far from the sea you were.

Her mum insisted that the ban – or "the break", as she was insisting on calling it – wasn't forever. Just to break whatever unhealthy patterns had led to them washing up on their own doorsteps half drowned in the middle of December. Lily could almost see it from her point of view. The cave had been stupid. But they knew that. They had learned their lesson. Swallowing and then throwing up a bellyful of salt water felt like a harsh enough punishment, so it seemed completely unfair that their parents were demanding more.

"Lily, what did I just say?"

Lily jerked her head up. She had been staring out of the window, wallowing in the unfairness of the situation. It took her a second to even remember she was in Ms Hanan's classroom, so the odds of her correctly guessing what had just been said were fairly slim. A couple of her classmates stifled giggles and Lily's face flushed. Sam, sitting a few rows away, offered a tiny sympathetic smile.

"Well?"

The sharpness in Ms Hanan's voice pierced Lily. "I don't know, miss. Sorry."

"OK. You might learn a little more if you keep your attention up here rather than out the window."

"Yes, miss." She picked up her pencil and scratched angry doodles into her jotter page.

"Jay, would you like to tell us what a rhyming couplet is?"

Jay started. He had been paying as little attention as Lily had. Sam's hand shot in the air.

"Please, miss. A rhyming couplet is two lines

of poetry that rhyme and usually have the same rhythm."

"I don't think I asked you, Sam."

Sam slumped. "Sorry, miss."

Ms Hanan sighed. "You're right, though. That's exactly what a rhyming couplet is. And what effect can a rhyming couplet have? Jay? Any ideas for this one?"

"Rhyming couplets give a poem structure."

"Good. And?"

"And they can be used to make a poem interesting. For dramatic effect."

His voice was flat and bored, as though he was reading notes from his hand. Ms Hanan raised an eyebrow slightly, but moved the class on.

Lily doodled aimlessly in her jotter as her classmates recited poetry around her. Someone recited something twee about the ocean and Lily rolled her eyes. The sea was never far from anyone's mind in Edge.

Suddenly a realisation that had been nagging at the edge of her mind hit her like a train. She sat bolt upright in her chair, snapping the lead of her pencil in shock.

> Those lost live on inside our hearts
> By time and tide, we're torn apart

The dedications from the two benches by the beach. They linked together. They formed a rhyming couplet. Their clues had led them to the right spot, they had just missed the next clue in the chain. She willed Sam and Jay to look her way but they were slumped in their seats, faces propped on their hands, scribbling just like she had been a few seconds ago. She spread her empty hands, looking around her as though a solution might present itself. It didn't.

Ms Hanan turned to write on the board. Lily saw her chance. She scribbled "BENCH DEDICATIONS ARE RHYMING COUPLETS" on a piece of paper, tore it from her jotter, balled it up and tossed it at Sam's lowered head. It bounced off gently and she let out a little cry. She finally caught Lily's eye and bent to retrieve the fallen note. She was too slow.

Ms Hanan scooped the note up from under her fingers and fixed Lily with an evil glare.

"Don't be shy, Lily. If you have an insight to share with Sam, I'm sure the rest of the class would love to hear it."

Lily sank down in her chair. Ms Hanan smoothed out the note and read it, her brow creasing slightly in confusion.

"Well, at least it looks school-related. Since you obviously find this topic so interesting, Lily, I'm sure you won't mind staying for after-school detention to do a little extra work. Sam and Jay, you too."

"But, miss!"

"Be quiet, Lily!"

The shout shocked Lily into silence. Her classmates diverted their eyes, embarrassed for her. Lily felt tears pricking at the back of her eyes. Even her favourite teacher had turned on her now. She stared at her jotter, trying very hard not to cry.

Twenty-Seven

At the last bell, everyone but Lily, Sam and Jay went home, laughing and yelling to each other. Ms Hanan closed the door, and as she turned to face them her face changed completely.

"I'm so sorry. Are you three all right?"

Lily blinked at her. "Are we ... what?"

Lily risked a glance at Sam and Jay, to see if they had any idea what was going on. They looked equally baffled.

"Er, yeah. I guess so."

"I couldn't think of any other way," said Ms Hanan.

"Any other way to what?"

Ms Hanan looked at Lily as though she was being dim. "Any other way to let the three of you see each other."

Lily's mouth dropped open. She exchanged astonished looks with her friends. All three of them started to laugh, and they ran for each other, leaping into a messy hug. A piece of Lily slotted back into place with a click.

She turned to look at Ms Hanan, whose eyes were sparkling with mischief.

"Why would you do this?"

Ms Hanan smiled and adjusted her hijab. "Oh, Lily. I've seen you when you were lonely and it was awful. I won't be the cause of that happening again. Now, go on, discuss your mysterious note and your mysterious rhyming couplet, whatever it is. I'd say we have about..." She checked her watch. "Oh, about an hour before anyone gets too suspicious and comes to check up on us."

She stepped behind her desk and sat down, pulling a pile of marking towards her. Lily took both of Sam's hands in hers and squeezed hard, before reaching one hand out to Jay and doing the same. They moved to the back of the classroom, pulling three chairs round one desk so they could speak without being heard.

"What did she mean about a rhyming couplet? What did your note say?"

"Remember when we followed the E arrow and found the bench by the sea? The weird dedication?"

Jay nodded. "Of course. But I thought we had decided that was a big load of nothing."

"It was. Or is. Well, sort of."

"Spit it out, woman," hissed Sam. "You're killing us here."

"It's not the full clue. It's only half of the next clue. Maybe less. I read the next bench along one day, but I didn't realise what it was until now. *'By time and tide, we're torn apart.'*"

Sam's eyes lit up. "*'Those lost live on inside our hearts; by time and tide, we're torn apart'.* A rhyming couplet! Lily, you're a genius."

"We need to get another look at those benches. There could be a whole poem out there."

"And if there's a whole poem..."

"It might tell us where to find Emily's diamond."

Twenty-Eight

Lily was desperate to get a look at the benches but her mum was still hovering far too close. She had decided that the mere sight of the sea would be enough to retraumatise Lily after her accident, so she was doing her best to keep them both far away from it.

Jay and Sam were having equally little luck. All they could do was wait for their parents to calm down and hope that the storm would pass soon.

Lily couldn't stop thinking about Ms Bright. For now, she was safe in hospital, but the town was abuzz with the happy news that she was getting better and would soon be home. She was awake and talking, but she obviously hadn't mentioned Snyde to anyone yet.

Lily was in town with her mum when she saw him again. He stepped into her path, startling her so much that she dropped her bag of groceries with a yelp. A box of eggs cracked messily on the pavement and oranges went skittering all across the road.

"Oh, Lily!" yelled her mum, running after a rogue orange.

Lily opened her mouth to shout, but before she could, Snyde pulled back his coat to show her what was hidden underneath. Tucked into his waistband was a serrated hunting knife. She blinked stupidly at him. For a moment, she almost laughed. The sight of the knife was too outrageous, too incongruous, with the sweet painted shutters and neat window boxes of Edge's main road. Snyde ran a calloused thumb along the knife's edge, darting his eyes at Lily's mum. Lily bit down on her lip hard.

Her mum came running back over, arms full of oranges. Snyde dropped his coat back into place, his eyes climbing over Lily's mum in a hungry way that made Lily want to kick him in the shins, knife or no knife. Lily bent to pick up her shopping bag, holding it out so her mum could replace the now slightly battered oranges. Snyde broke into a smile. It made Lily feel sick.

"So this must be Lily's mum," he said, holding his hand out. "I don't believe we've met."

Lily's mum shifted her shopping to one side so she could shake his hand. "No, I don't believe we have. Mr...?"

"Snyde. I'm ... one of Lily's teachers."

"Oh! I thought I had met all of Lily's teachers. What subject do you teach?"

Snyde grinned horribly at Lily. "Ancient history."

Lily glared at him.

"Actually, would you mind if I borrow Lily for a moment? I had a question about one of her assignments."

Lily looked up at her mum, willing her to understand that they should both be getting as far away from this man as possible. Her mum smiled. "Of course. I need to nip into a couple more shops anyway. Lily, do you want to meet me in the bakery once you're done?"

Lily's heart sank. Her mum was officially less perceptive than Costello. She watched her go with pleading eyes and then turned to face Snyde, trying to look fierce. He stuck a cigarette in his mouth.

"So," he said pleasantly, "I hear that poor Ms Bright

suffered a nasty accident."

"We know it wasn't an accident, and soon so will everyone. Haven't you heard? She's awake."

Lily immediately wished she hadn't said that. But Snyde just laughed.

"If she was going to talk, she'd have done it by now. And soon she won't have the chance. Amazing how dangerous these small towns can be, isn't it? Something that looks completely harmless can turn out to be quite the little thorn in your side."

"Is that what you think me and my friends are? A thorn? You're the one who won't leave us alone."

"Lily, I wouldn't even know your name if you hadn't been poking around where you don't belong."

"What do you want?"

The strike of a match, the glow of a flame catching, the cloud of smoke engulfing his face for a second. "I want no more and no less than what is rightfully mine. There is an item of significant ... sentimental value to me. I simply want to make sure it doesn't fall into the wrong hands."

"The diamond."

Snyde's head jerked. "So you do know about the diamond."

"You'll never get it. Ms Bright told us the story. It was being saved for someone sharp of brain and true of heart and that's definitely not you."

Snyde laughed, then spat. "I knew it. I knew she had lied to me."

"Ms Bright didn't lie to you. She doesn't even believe that the diamond exists."

"I'm not talking about your precious Ms Bright."

Lily's heart lurched. "Her mum. Joanie."

"She thought she was so clever, laughing at me, insisting that she didn't know where it was. All the while saving it for her precious girls. Well, she didn't laugh for long. I always knew it would be worth my while to keep an eye on this little place. Flotsam always washes up eventually."

"You're wrong. Ms Bright doesn't have the diamond. She doesn't even think it's real. Or she didn't, before you smacked her on the head. She might have changed her mind now."

"Where is it?" he hissed, seething into her face.

Smoke curls escaped from his mouth, stinging Lily's eyes, clinging horribly to her hair.

"I don't know! I don't know, I don't know, I don't know!"

He pointed a finger into her face. "I hope for your sake that's true. You listen to me. I am going to find that diamond and if you or your little friends get in my way, well ... you've seen how accidents can happen. I heard that you all had a bit of a close call recently. It would be terrible for something like that to happen again."

An icy finger ran up Lily's spine. "You don't scare me."

Snyde grinned. "Then why are you shaking so hard?"

Lily stuffed her hands into her coat pockets and jutted her chin at him defiantly. "We're going to stop you, you know. Terrible men like you always get what you deserve."

He grinned, nodded at the book poking out of Lily's pocket. "Maybe in your little storybooks. But not out here in the real world. Out here, you're just a powerless little girl. You're nothing."

"No, *you're* nothing. A greedy, heartless, shadowy, murdery nothing." She almost yelled the last word.

"My, my, we are feeling brave today, aren't we? Stay out of my way. Or I'll—" He straightened up suddenly, pinching out his cigarette and stashing it in his pocket. Lily turned.

Her mum was heading back towards them, wrestling an enormous baguette into a bag.

Snyde raised his voice. "The important thing to remember about history, Lily, is that it repeats itself." A sly smile crept over his face as he darted his eyes back towards Lily's mum. "Always."

Lily wished she could think of some smart comment, some brilliant comeback, but her voice was frozen, lodged painfully in her throat.

"There we go," said Lily's mum. "We're all done. Are you ready to head home, Lily?"

"Yes," said Lily. "We're done."

"Mr Snyde, I don't suppose you'd like to join us for some lunch?"

Lily almost screamed.

"What a lovely offer, Ms Hargan, but no thank you.

Maybe another time. It's a small town; I'm sure we'll see each other again very soon."

He threw Lily a triumphant look and sloped off. Lily drew in a long, deep breath, trying to steady her chest. Her mum laughed.

"Blimey, he was a bit intense, wasn't he? Is he always like that?"

"I hate him."

Lily's mum laughed again, ruffling Lily's curls. "My little warrior woman. I shouldn't have raised you with such a flare for the dramatic. Come on, home for lunch."

They headed back to their house, the shadow of Snyde hanging over Lily all the way.

Twenty-Nine

Lily, Jay and Sam sat cross-legged on the floor of Ms Hanan's classroom, organising enormous piles of books and stationery while Lily filled them in on her conversation with Snyde.

"Ugh, what a creep," said Sam.

"It was awful," said Lily.

"So he thinks Ms Bright has been looking for the diamond?" said Jay.

Lily slotted a book into the shelf by her head. "Honestly, I'm not even sure if he knows what he's talking about. He thinks everyone is out to get him and that everyone is trying to steal something from him."

Sam scoffed. "I for one think we should definitely steal something from him."

Jay hefted a little pile of books on to his lap. "He really did it. He really killed Ms Bright's mum."

"And that's why Emily had to disappear."

"We need to solve the treasure hunt," said Lily. "The story about the diamond started all of this. Maybe whatever we find at the end of the clues will help us to finish it."

"What if we get to the end and it's actually an enormous diamond?"

"What if we get to the end and it's a trap? We don't even know who sent the museum ticket to Ms Bright."

"We need to get a look at those benches," said Sam.

"But how?" asked Jay. "My mum is still following me around like a shadow."

Sam grinned. "I think it's time to start breaking some rules."

It took forever for Lily's mum to fall asleep. Lily had been afraid that she would doze off herself but there was no chance of that. Her whole body fizzed with anticipation. She tried to read, tried singing songs in her head, tried to do anything but stare at the hand on her clock as crawled its way round. Seconds stretched into minutes, minutes into hours, and Lily genuinely worried that she might lose her mind if she didn't stop watching the time pass.

Finally, at two in the morning, the house was quiet.

Lily had gone to bed dressed, pulling her quilt around her chin so that when her mum came to check on her and switch off the lamp, she wouldn't be able to tell. Her boots and her warmest jumpers were laid out on the chair, a dressing gown draped over them to hide them.

She pushed back her covers and slipped out of bed.

She wriggled into two jumpers and then pulled on three extra pairs of socks. The jumpers made her arms stiff and she struggled to reach her toes. She should have done this the other way round. Nocturnal sneaking was not something she was particularly experienced in. She laced her boots, squeezed her jacket over the layers of jumpers and jammed her hat on to her head. Her jacket rustled as she moved, and she froze again, listening out for any sound of movement from her mum's room. Nothing. She checked her pockets. Torch, keys, paper, pencil, three chocolate biscuits she had stashed away earlier. She was ready.

She eased open her window. Cold air whistled in through the gap, making Lily shiver, even through all her layers. It was absolutely dark outside, the kind of dark that didn't exist in the city. She could hear the faint crashing of the sea, and as she slid herself over the edge of the windowsill she was seized with irrational panic that the water was right beneath her, waiting for her to fall. She knew, of course, that what lay beneath her dangling feet was her garden, but it still took her a few minutes to make herself move from the safety of the windowsill.

She reached out an arm tentatively, wishing she'd had a chance to practise this in the light. Right at the edge of her reach, her fingertips grazed the drainpipe. She leaned a little further, shifting her balance into the dark, trying not to panic. Her fingers closed round its rough surface. With her other hand she wedged a book under the window, making sure it wouldn't close behind her and lock her out.

She tightened her grip on the drainpipe and reached out with her foot, looking for a hold. Her balance shifted a little too far and she swung from the windowsill, tearing the skin on her palm and colliding with the pipe, sending a magnificent clang vibrating through the night. She froze, waiting for the lights to come on, for the yelling to start. At least sneaking out to solve a treasure hunt and keep an ancient diamond from a murderer was unlikely to be the first of her mum's suspicions.

The house stayed silent. She peered into the dark, wondering if Sam was stuck up a different drainpipe just a few metres away. She couldn't see anything. She climbed down the pipe, wincing at every metallic scraping sound. Her foot hit a patch of ice and slipped. She fell, fortunately only a metre or so; her fall broken by her mum's hibernating rose bush. Lily shook leaves from her hair. Her mum was not going to be happy about that.

She looked up at her open window. It looked almost close enough to touch. She couldn't believe it had taken so long to come such a short distance. She scowled at the drainpipe, contemplated giving it a kick, but decided it probably wasn't worth the risk. She straightened her hat, zipped her jacket up under her chin and headed out into the dark, feeling her way along the row of garden walls.

She didn't dare switch on her torch until she rounded the corner away from her house, and then she kept it pointed downwards, lighting her path, looking out for errant cobblestones or slippery patches. The main road appeared ahead of her and she followed the pinprick glimmer of the street lights, like a sailor navigating dark waters by the stars. The road was completely deserted.

It was eerie, the familiar window fronts shuttered and blank, her footsteps the only sound on the normally bustling street. She bent as she passed over the compass at the crossroad, touching the carved heart for luck. The light died away again as she left the main road. After the glow of the street lights, the dark seemed even deeper and more impenetrable than before. She could hear the sea close by now and went slowly, terrified that at any moment she would step over a cliff edge.

"Lily!"

The whisper came from nearby. She stopped and swung the beam of her torch around. Sam clicked her torch on and waved, guiding Lily to the bench.

She was sitting with her shoulders hunched against the cold, Costello huddled between her knees.

"You brought Costello?" said Lily, stroking the dog's ears.

Sam shrugged. "It seemed like the easiest way to stop him whining and waking up the whole house after I was gone."

"You just walked out the front door?"

"Of course. What did you do?"

"Oh. Er, same."

Lily was glad it was dark so Sam couldn't see her blush. She sat down beside her friend, squeezing in close for warmth.

"So have you read the dedications yet?"

"Not yet. It felt like something we should do together."

Lily nodded, and then remembered that Sam couldn't see her.

"What time is it?"

Sam was wearing a ridiculous glow-in-the-dark watch, which Lily had often made fun of. Now she was very glad of it.

"Quarter to three."

"Where's Jay? It's not like him to be late."

"Maybe he couldn't get out."

"How long do we wait?"

"Let's give him until three, see how cold we feel by then."

Lily already felt completely frozen. Sam linked her arm through Lily's and they huddled close. The minute hand of Sam's watch had just touched the twelve when the light of Jay's torch came bobbing towards them. Lily flashed hers on and off a few times to let him know where they were.

"I'm so sorry, my brother woke up as I was getting ready to leave. I had to pay him not to tell on me."

"Brothers," sympathised Sam.

"Are we ready?"

"Let's do it."

Three shaking torch beams pointed to the brass plaque screwed into the bench.

"Those lost live on inside our hearts," read Lily.

"By time and tide, we're torn apart", continued Sam, turning to give Lily a warm smile.

Nervously, they moved to the third bench in the row. *"When oceans calm and danger's gone,"* read Jay.

"You'll be the light to guide me home!" Lily turned to her friends, a triumphant grin lighting her face.

"You were right! A pair of couplets!"

"Read it again. I want to write it down in case I forget," said Lily, pulling her paper and pencil from her pocket. Jay held his torch above her, while Sam reread the poem. Costello sat down on top of Lily's feet, shivering hard and giving them all doleful looks. Lily scribbled the poem down and stuck the paper back in her pocket.

"It still sounds religious to me," said Jay. "Light and guidance and all that. That's really churchy."

Lily frowned. She felt as though the answer was lurking at the edge of her mind, just out of reach.

Thirty

"Lily!"

Lily jolted upright and leapt from her bed, tangling up her bed sheets and sprawling face first on to the ground. She immediately started shivering. It was freezing. She looked around and saw that her window was still open, propped up with the book she had left jammed in it last night. She yanked the book out and clicked the window closed, just as her mum marched into the room.

"I've been yelling for ages, didn't you hear me? You're going to be late for school."

Lily became dimly aware that her alarm was going off and blearily slapped the top of the clock to switch it off. She yelped as she saw the time.

"It's absolutely freezing in here. Is your window letting out all the heat?"

"Don't know," said Lily, grabbing pieces of clothing at random and shoving them on.

"Well, see if it warms up. If not, I'll get someone to come and look at it."

"Fine," said Lily, rubbing sleep from her eyes with one hand and piling things into her school bag with the other.

She skidded into school just as the bell rang and would probably have made it on time had she not collided heavily with Ms Bruce. She bounced off and almost lost her footing. Ms Bruce looked down at the tiny asteroid of a child who had crashed into her and her face twisted with distaste.

"Lily Hargan. There is no running in the hallways."

Lily tried to look normal. "Sorry, Ms Bruce. I didn't want to be late."

"Well, if you arrive a little earlier, you can be on time without breaking the rules."

Ms Bruce grimaced, as though this interaction was confirming every suspicion she held about Lily. She bent down, pressing her face close to Lily's.

"Do you know," she said, raising an eyebrow, "that you are wearing two different shoes?"

Lily looked down. She was right. They were both black shoes, at least – relatively similar, but undeniably halves of two different pairs of shoes.

Her face flamed. She squared her shoulders.

"It's a new look I'm trying out. Thank you for noticing."

"May I suggest that in future you save such experimentations for outside of school?"

"Of course, Ms Bruce. Sorry."

"Off you go. You're late."

Lily made a suitably chastised face until her back was turned to Ms Bruce and then allowed herself an extravagant eye-roll. She made her apologies to Ms Hanan and slid exhausted into her seat. Sam and Jay offered weak smiles. They looked terrible. That must be what Lily looked like too.

At break, Lily made her way back to Ms Hanan's classroom. Sam and Jay were already there, slumped in chairs. Ms Hanan was pouring tea.

Sam lifted her head from the desk and smiled at Lily. "I like your shoes. It's a bold look."

Lily laughed and slid in beside her. "Big words from someone who has their shirt on inside out."

Sam looked down. "Oh no." She reached over and smacked Jay on the shoulder. "Thanks for letting me know, Captain Observant."

Jay shrugged. "Sam, my eyes are barely open. Of course I didn't notice."

"Are you three all right?" asked Ms Hanan. "You're starting to worry me a little."

"Don't worry," said Sam. "We're just a bit preoccupied."

"We're solving a mystery," added Jay.

"I see."

Lily pulled the poem from her pocket and placed it in the middle of the table. They rubbed their eyes and leaned forward to look.

Ms Hanan laughed. "Oh, I see, it's like a riddle! Don't get me wrong, I'm thrilled that you're taking such an interest in rhyming couplets but not so thrilled that it appears to be keeping you up all night."

"A riddle?" said Lily. "Does that mean you know what the answer is?"

"I think so. I could have a guess anyway."

"What is it?" demanded Sam.

"Now, where would be the fun in that? I thought you wanted to solve the mystery, whatever it is."

"Ms Hanan, this is important."

Ms Hanan folded her arms and smiled in amusement. "You can get it, I promise."

"Is it to do with a church?" asked Jay.

"Hmm, I see why you might think that but it's not what I'm thinking of. You're going too abstract. Remember Occam's razor."

"What's Occam's razor?" asked Lily.

"It means that the simplest solution is often the correct one," said Jay. "But what does that have to do with the poem?"

"It means that you're thinking too hard. Go simple. Think literally," said Ms Hanan.

Lily turned the words over in her mind. *Simple. Simple. Simple.* Her head jerked up and she barked with surprised laughter.

"Of course! We *were* thinking too hard! The answer was right in front of us the whole time."

"What is it?"

Lily turned triumphantly to look out of the classroom window. "The lighthouse."

Thirty-One

The rain had just started to fall when Lily heard the news that Ms Bright was to come home. The town had been gearing itself up for a storm all week, the sky remaining dark all through the day and clouds gathered low in the sky, like a lid on a pot that was about to boil.

Despite the cold, the air felt stuffy and oppressive. Lily knew that something was coming. She could feel it prickling her skin, beating at the back of her mind.

That morning, at long last, the first freezing raindrops had started to fall. Lily's mum looked up as they tapped on to the kitchen window and breathed a sigh of relief.

"Thank goodness. We need a good storm. This town has been going crazy all week."

The rain was falling slowly for now, just a few fat drops spattering on to the glass, but Lily could see the sky turning darker, the sea reflecting its angry bruised purple. Lily's mum smiled. She had always loved thunderstorms and had passed that love on to Lily. Often they would sit together, candles lit, playing cards or board games, warm under a blanket, enjoying the spectacle of a storm passing over the city. But Lily had a bad feeling about this one. Maybe it was being so close to the sea that was making her anxious.

"Oh, I almost forgot – I heard some good news today," said Lily's mum, stirring the pot on the stove. "Ms Bright is coming home."

Lily knocked over her cup, spilling water all over the kitchen table.

"Oh, for goodness' sake, Lily. Would you be careful?"

"She's coming home? When?"

"Tomorrow, I think. She's much better. Isn't that lovely? She'll be home in time for Christmas."

Lily tried to quiet her mind. "Yes, that's lovely."

She grabbed a tea towel and mopped up the water on the table. A boom of thunder made her jump, rattling the window in its frame. Her mum grinned.

"There we go, it's getting started."

Lily sat down and waited a few minutes, to let her mum's mind wander away from Ms Bright. Then she made a pained face, bolted to the bathroom and sat on the edge of the bath making her most conspicuous retching sounds. Her mum knocked gently on the door.

"Lily? Lily, are you all right?"

Lily flushed the toilet and ran her hands under the cold tap, patting water on to her face to make herself look clammy and ill. She opened the bathroom door, adopting her most pathetic face.

"I don't feel very well."

Lily's mum felt her forehead, withdrawing her hand with a grimace at its damp surface.

"Oh, sweetheart. Do you need to go to the doctor?"

Lily shook her head. "I don't think so. I think I just want to lie down for a while. Is that OK?"

"Of course. Come on, let's get you tucked up."

Lily was bundled into bed with a hot-water bottle and a glass of ginger ale. She lay still for a while. It was cosy in bed, even more so with the storm ramping up outside. She could just stay here. She pulled the cover up over her head. It was no use. She had to go.

She kicked the covers off and tiptoed to the other

side of the room, where her warm clothes from her last night-time adventure were still lying discarded. She congratulated herself on being so usefully messy. She put on her socks and shoes first this time, before pulling on her jumpers. Her raincoat was yellow, which wasn't exactly the best colour for being inconspicuous, but by the looks of the sky outside she was definitely going to need it.

She slid her window open and manoeuvred herself out on to the drainpipe. The cut on her palm opened up again. It was easier to climb in the light but the rain and the cold had made the pipe even slippier. She was glad when her feet thumped into the wreckage of her mum's rose bush.

She pressed herself against the wall of the house, ducking under the kitchen window. She prayed that no one would walk past and wave to her. An enormous gust of wind buffeted the house, slapping Lily with drops of sea spray.

She hopped over the wall separating her house and Sam's and picked up a handful of gravel. She looked up at Sam's bedroom window, weighing the stones in her palm. This was not playing to her skill set. She wasn't exactly known for her delicate touch.

She took a deep breath, prayed that she wouldn't hurl the stone hard enough to break the window and tossed it upwards. It dinked off the glass and fell. Lily waited. No response. She tossed another stone. Still no response. She huffed and drew back for a third throw. She launched the pebble. As it left her hand, Sam pulled the window open. She had to dodge out of the way of the oncoming projectile and waved her hands at Lily in the universal sign for "knock it off".

Lily beckoned her to come down. Sam widened her eyes and gestured at the sky. Lily gave her a pleading look. Sam did a full-body eye-roll and disappeared from the window for a second. Lily moved back to the garden wall, crouching behind it, just in case her mum happened to look out of their window and spot her.

Lily's heart leapt into her mouth as Sam reappeared, a bed sheet in hand, and knotted one corner of it round her window frame. She gave it a hard tug, made a terrified face at Lily and dropped the other end down the side of the house. It didn't quite reach the ground, but it came close enough.

Lily held her breath as her friend gripped the sheet and started to slowly shimmy down. She reached the bottom, her feet about a metre from the ground. She let go, landing on her feet but overbalancing and falling on to her back with an irritated "Oof!".

Lily ran to check she was all right but was beaten by Costello, who decided that the best way to be helpful was to sit on Sam's chest and lick her face. Sam flailed ineffectively underneath him.

"Get off! Stupid dog! I'll have you made into a hat!"

Lily smothered a laugh and grabbed Costello's collar, tugging him off Sam and shoving him with difficulty back through the doggy door. Sam sat up, face gleaming, the back of her head dusted with leaves.

"This had better be good, Hargan."

"It's the opposite. Ms Bright is coming home."

Sam's eyes widened. "When?"

"Tomorrow, according to my mum. And when she gets out, she's going to run."

Sam shivered. "If Snyde doesn't get to her first."

"Exactly. So if we're going to solve this mystery, it needs to be tonight. Or she'll be gone and we'll never be able to tell her what we found."

Sam looked out towards the sea, waves angrily battering the shore, clouds whipping overhead. "Sure. Of course it needs to be tonight."

Lily's heart felt heavy. She thought of the museum as they'd last found it. The shining glass, every item lovingly restored. Just waiting for someone to come back for them.

"We can't let her give it all up again. It's just like she said. *This* is her home. We need to find out what happened. Then maybe she can stay."

Sam nodded. "We need to go and get Jay." She pulled her phone from her pocket. "I got this back today. I have officially rejoined the modern world. Only problem is, I don't think Jay has."

Sam withheld her mobile number and rang Jay's landline. With a bit of luck, Jay would pick up. The phone rang twice and Lily groaned as Jay's mum answered. Sam was silent for a second, then she nodded at Lily smugly and covered the microphone of her phone with her scarf.

"Hello, this is Ms Hanan from school. Would it be possible to speak to Jay regarding a school assignment, please?"

Her voice was high and ridiculous. Lily had never heard anyone sound less like a real adult. She had to stuff her hat in her mouth to keep from laughing. Sam punched her shoulder, her face also full of the giggles. She waited for a few seconds.

"Oh, hello, Jay, it's your favourite teacher in the whole wide world." A few seconds, then Sam said in her normal voice, "Of course it's not Ms Hanan, you clown, it's me. Listen, you need to get out of the house. Ms Bright is getting out of hospital. Meet us at the bench in ten minutes." Pause. "I don't know, climb out of your window. That's what Lily and I did. No, seriously. We did. OK. See you soon."

She zipped the phone back into her pocket and rolled her eyes at Lily. "Honestly, boys are such cowards. You ready?"

"Not even close."

"Me neither. Let's go."

They jumped the wall, leaving Sam's bed sheet blowing in the wind behind them. By the time her dads spotted it, it would be far too late.

Thirty-Two

The waves were coming over the top of the sea wall
by the time the three had made their way to the
bench. Lily was soaked through, despite her raincoat.
The wind threatened to pick them up and toss them
over the wall and they bent double as they walked,
driving themselves into the storm. They held hands,
salty, slippery fingers anchoring them to each other.

"This is crazy!" yelled Jay.

The wind whipped his words away, the bellowing
thunder drowning him out. Neither of the girls heard
him. A flash of lightning forked across the sky. Lily
counted one, two – boom! The storm was right on top
of them. A wave came flying over the wall, engulfing
them all for a second. Lily screamed, immediately
regretting it as her mouth filled with seawater.
She spluttered, spitting it out and scrubbing at her
tongue with the back of her hand.

The lighthouse was at the far end of the promenade,
on the tip of a craggy outcrop of rocks. Coated
with seaweed and slippery at the best of times, the

path that stretched before them now was almost impassable. They made their way in tiny sideways steps, like a parade of crabs. Every so often they'd have to stop and turn their backs to the sea, bracing themselves against a particularly vicious barrage of waves. Lily had never been so thoroughly drenched in her whole life.

The lighthouse, which seemed postcard-tiny and adorable from the beach, was enormous up close. It towered above them, its surface furred with soaking moss, creaking ominously with every furious gust of wind. Lily put her hand up to her eyes and craned her neck back, peering up towards the darkened lamp of the lighthouse.

"It's the perfect place to hide something," she yelled over the storm.

"I know," yelled Sam. "Hiding in plain sight."

They felt their way round the bottom of the lighthouse until they came to what must have once been a door. It was encrusted with barnacles and rust, coated in the same slimy film as the rest of the building. Lily ran her palm over the surface, her fingers eventually picking out the shape of an enormous metal ring. She pulled it out with a sickening sucking sound, turned it and yanked. The door stayed firmly closed. She tugged again and again. No joy. It was completely stuck. Sam and Jay reached around her, closing their fingers round the ring. Sam grimaced.

"Eugh! That's so slimy."

Lily wrinkled her nose in agreement, before bracing one foot against the wall.

"On the count of three? One, two, three!"

They pulled as one, throwing their full combined body weight behind it. With an agonising screech, the door opened just a little. Just a little was enough. They wriggled through the narrow gap into the lighthouse.

The sound of the storm was muffled inside, the howling wind sounding mournful and far away.

"We're probably the first people to step inside here in about a hundred years," whispered Sam.

Lily pulled her torch from the pocket of her waterproof and pointed it at the spiral steps in front of them. They had probably been a deathtrap when they were brand new and the years since had not been kind to them. They were narrow and twisting, some of them rusted all the way through. Lily put her hand on the railing and pulled. It swayed under her fingers. This did not fill her with confidence. She turned back to her friends.

"Slowly," they agreed.

Lily went first, gripping the railing. Even a faulty railing was better than nothing on such steep steps. She prodded at each step tentatively with her toe before putting her weight on it, skipping a few steps that shuddered under her. Looking up made her feel dizzy, so she focused on each step in front of her, trying not to think about the storm raging around them, making the old structure groan under its onslaught.

"These circles are starting to make me feel sick," said Sam.

"Agreed," said Lily. "How did anyone do this?"

She completed another tight circle and stopped dead, making Sam crash into the back of her with a little cry.

"What is it? Why have you stopped?"

Lily leaned out of the way, to show Sam and Jay what was in front of her. It was a door. She shoved it open, stepping tentatively through.

"Oh, wow," she said, unable to hide the glee in her voice.

"Is it a diamond?" said Sam, scrambling through after her.

"Not that good. But look."

They were in the lighthouse keeper's living quarters. The wooden boards of the floor must have been polished once but were now dull with age and salt. The patterned rug was moth-eaten and worn. An armchair stood in the corner, its upholstery spilling out and the remains of what looked like a seagull's nest instead of a seat. There was a tiny stove, a cast-iron kettle, a pile of long-forgotten books.

"This is the coolest thing I've ever seen," said Lily.

Rain pelted the window on the far side of the room. Lily wiped the dirt from its surface and peered out. Nothing but black.

"This must be beautiful when it's light."

"And when we're not in the middle of an enormous storm," said Jay.

As if to emphasise his point, the building gave an emphatic shudder.

"OK," said Lily. "We're assuming something is hidden here. Either another clue or…"

She could hardly bring herself to believe it, never mind say it aloud.

"Or a diamond the size of a man's fist," said Sam wryly.

"Right. So we have to look around."

They pulled open drawers, and looked inside the stove and the cast-iron kettle. They pulled back the rug and thumbed the soggy books. They looked behind the picture frames on the wall for secret safes. Despite its abandoned condition, Lily couldn't shake the feeling that they were rifling through someone's belongings – that at any second the lighthouse keeper could burst in and demand to know just what they thought they were doing. The room was small and it didn't take them long to search. They found nothing.

"I guess we keep going," said Jay.

"I guess we do."

Lily crossed to the far side of the room and opened the door. She immediately regretted complaining about the spiral stairs. In front of her, leading upwards, was a long wooden ladder. She looked behind her and saw her own pained expression reflected on the faces of her friends. She placed a hand gently on the rung in front of her. The wood was damp and swollen. A splinter lodged itself in her hand as she gripped. She stepped apprehensively on to the bottom rung. It groaned underneath her but held. She stuck her torch between her teeth and jerked her head at her friends. The three started to climb.

The sound of the storm grew again as they climbed and Lily was aware that it was getting colder. Her torch illuminated a wooden trapdoor in the ceiling, warped and bent in its frame. She braced her shoulder against it and shoved, disgorging a shower of lichen and wood shavings into the upturned faces of her friends. They spluttered beneath her.

"Sorry," she said round the handle of her torch.

The trapdoor creaked open and fell away with a slam. Lily pulled herself up through the gap, then reached down to help Sam and Jay. She wiped the handle of her torch and swung it around. They were in the beacon room of the lighthouse. Darkness was the only thing visible through the filthy windows on one side; on the other, the lights of the town glimmered in the distance. Lily felt as though they had climbed forever, but the movement in the blackness outside worryingly suggested that the waves were now coming this high, battering against the glass.

In the centre of the room was the old lighthouse beacon. Nestled inside, where there should have been a lamp, was a diamond.

Thirty-Three

"Oh, my goodness," breathed Lily.

She tried to take a step forward but felt as though she was rooted to the spot. She pointed her quivering torch beam at the diamond. It caught the light and tossed it around the dark space in dancing, multicoloured fragments. An enormous wave slammed into the glass behind them, but the three barely noticed. Sam's hand landed on Lily's shoulder, giving her a gentle shove.

"Go on," she whispered, not really sure why she was whispering. "Go and get it."

Lily shuffled forward. The diamond winked mischievously in the moving light. She reached out and pulled the jewel from its resting place. It was heavy and cold to the touch. Lily turned to her friends, struck with astonishment.

"It's a diamond," she said.

"It's a real diamond," said Jay.

"It's a real diamond!" yelled Sam.

They started to scream, wildly laughing and yelling

and leaping up and down, ignoring the protests of the ancient wood underneath them.

"We need to get this to Ms Bright. Once the adults see it, they'll know we're telling the truth. They'll just have to believe us about everything else."

"Do you think so?" came a voice from behind them.

They spun in unison and screamed. The storm had grown so loud that they hadn't heard the wrench of the door being yanked open, the creak of the ladder underneath. Snyde pulled himself up into the beacon room, his eyes lighting up hungrily as he spotted the diamond. The three children cowered against the glass, circling the room, keeping the beacon between Snyde and themselves. Lily cradled the diamond protectively against her chest.

"Yes," he hissed. "I knew it. Sweet, lying little Joanie McCrae. Clever of her to hide it up here for her girls. Clever of you to find it. It's a shame you won't get to keep it."

Sam stepped forward. Lily shot her a panicked glance. Sam gave her a tiny smile. Her face was white, her eyes trained forward. Her hand was moving in her pocket.

"What are you going to do?" she said. "Just kill us and leave us in this lighthouse for someone to find?"

Snyde laughed unpleasantly. "It's taken over a hundred years for someone to find a diamond left up here. I don't think anyone is going to come and find you. Your parents will be burying empty caskets, just like poor Emily and Caitlyn had to with their mother."

"You didn't kill Emily's mum up here. There's no body."

"I didn't have to drag her all the way up here. I had her row out to meet me by the caves, on a night very much like this one. She looked me right in the eye, swore that she had no idea where the diamond was. I still remember the look on her face as I pushed her."

Lily's eyes filled. The sea bellowed all around them, waves pummelling the windows of the beacon room. She had never been so afraid in her whole stupid life. Over Snyde's shoulder, out by the lights of the town, Lily saw something that made her heart lift. Snyde frowned and turned to see what Lily was looking at.

A tiny flashing blue light was visible, winding its way along the seafront road towards them. Snyde strode forward, grabbing Sam by the wrist and wrenching her hand out of her pocket. She was gripping her phone, a call to the police active on its screen. Snyde seized it furiously and threw it to the ground, smashing the heel of his boot into its screen. He pulled back his coat and drew the long knife from his belt. Sam struggled to pull her wrist from his grip but he held on firmly, laughing. She lashed out with her arms and legs, trying to scratch his face, kick his shins, anything to make him let go. Behind him, the blue light crawled towards them, agonisingly slowly.

Snyde held Sam at arm's length and glanced backwards, laughing.

"It was a good idea, little girl, I'll give you that. But it's not going to work. By the time they get here, I'll be long gone. No one is coming to save you."

Lily realised he was right. No one was coming to save them. She'd just have to do it herself. Snyde saw her smile and frowned, his confusion staying the knife. Lily turned to face the black sea and coiled herself backwards. Snyde's features twisted in rage and he let go of Sam, throwing himself at Lily. He was too late. Lily threw the diamond with all of her strength, shattering the window of the beacon room and sending the jewel spiralling into the darkness.

"No!" screamed Snyde, rushing towards the broken window.

A wave smashed through the room, knocking them all off their feet, sending Snyde's knife spinning away from him. Lily gasped for breath, spitting out freezing seawater and grasping for her friends in the confusion. Below them, the light of the police car drew near.

"We need to get out of here!" she yelled.

Snyde was frantically grabbing for his knife, wiping stinging saltwater from his eyes and screaming all manner of threats. They scrambled down the ladder, feet slipping on the soaking rungs, falling more than climbing. Lily pulled her friends into the lighthouse keeper's chambers, slamming the door closed behind them and tipping the bookshelf over to create a barricade. She turned back as they reached the second door, just in time to see Snyde's knife come hacking through the rotten wood.

"Go!" she yelled. "Go! Go!"

They clattered down the spiral stairs, round and round for what seemed like forever. Lily screamed as her foot smashed clean through a stair and she fell, wrenching her wrist, smacking into the back of Sam, sending them all crashing downwards. She landed, winded, on all fours and realised with a cry of relief that they had fallen to the bottom. Snyde's steps were still ringing behind them. She grabbed each of her friends by the scruff of their necks and dragged them back to their feet, all three of them bursting out of the lighthouse and into the freezing air outside.

Lily collapsed on to her hands and knees, coughing up seawater and gasping for breath. She could hear someone calling her name, could just about make out some very angry-looking parents and one very anxious-looking librarian running towards them. A pair of extraordinarily shiny shoes bolted past her and she looked up at the broad, unamused face of

Sergeant Bruce. It didn't seem like the time for *I told you so*. She smiled thinly at him and rolled on to her back. She just needed to rest for a minute. The wind continued to howl and batter the coast with waves but above her, Lily could see the storm starting to break. She could see the stars.

Thirty-Four

All three of them had terrible colds. Lily, it transpired, had actually broken her wrist, an enormous cuff of bruised and swollen flesh rising round it in just a few hours. She was rather proud of it. She thought it made her look fierce. They had all been grounded until the end of the century.

Snyde was arrested. Sam's quick thinking meant that the police had heard his entire confession. Even Sergeant Bruce couldn't ignore that.

Ms Bright had been on her way home, having discharged herself from hospital when she had spotted the torchlight at the top of the lighthouse. Ignoring her taxi driver's protestations, she had clambered out of the car to see what was going on. She had been completely astonished to see an enormous diamond come flying out of the beacon room – and even more astonished to see it hit the ground and shatter. She had been sitting dumbfounded on the rocks, picking shards of broken glass from her hair, when Sergeant Bruce and the parents arrived.

All things considered, Lily was astounded when her mum agreed that they could go to Sam's parents' New Year's Eve party. Their annual party was world famous – well, town-famous anyway. They crammed far too many people into their house, welcoming guests, friends and all manner of miscellaneous newcomers, before decanting on to the beach for singing and a frankly irresponsible amount of fireworks.

Lily threw herself at Sam the second they were in the door, Costello leaping excitedly on to them, knocking them into a giggling heap on the floor. It took Lily a second to place what was different.

"Sam," she said. "You're wearing a dress."

Sam gave a smug little shrug. "Multitudes, darling. We all of us contain multitudes."

Lily grinned. "You sound just like your dad."

Jay piled on top of them, picking them up and spinning them around. His mum looked as though she might have an aneurysm. The house was packed, Lily constantly thinking that they couldn't fit another person in and constantly being proven wrong. It seemed like the whole town was here. In the kitchen, Sergeant Bruce and his sister were complaining about the various problems with modern youth. Lily gave them a wide berth. On the landing, Ms Bright was excitedly admiring Ms Hanan's sparkling engagement ring. In the living room, Lily's mum was bent double, tears of laughter streaming down her face as Sam's papa impersonated Ms Bruce. Everyone was happy.

Lily was sitting on the stairs, looking for a little quiet. The music thrummed through the wall and she leaned her head against it, feeling the gentle vibration move through her. She almost didn't hear the tentative knock on the door. She looked around but all of the adults seemed to be otherwise occupied. She hoisted herself off the step and opened the door. A woman was hovering on the path, hands buried deep in her pockets, an anxious look on her face that seemed at odds with the party raging inside. Lily didn't recognise her, but she supposed she probably didn't know everyone in town just yet.

"I'm sorry, I'm not sure if I'm in the right place."

Lily grinned. "You almost definitely are. Everyone in the world is inside."

The woman returned a ghost of a smile. "I'm looking for—"

"Caitlyn," came a voice from behind Lily.

Lily's mouth fell open.

"Emily." The woman stepped round Lily, her hands grasping for Ms Bright's. "Did you mean what you said? Is it really over?"

Ms Bright smiled at her sister, her eyes shimmering. "It's over. We're finally safe."

Caitlyn threw herself into Ms Bright's arms and they stood there for a long, long time. Sam wandered into the hall and her eyes lit up as she took in the two women on the doorstep.

"Ms Bright, I didn't know you had a girlfriend!" she exclaimed.

Lily snorted.

"No, this is—" began Ms Bright.

"Come in! Come and join the party! I'm Sam, I live here."

She thrust a hand at the bemused Caitlyn.

"It's nice to meet you, Sam. I'm Caitlyn."

"Ha! That's so weird, Ms Bright's sister is…"

Sam finally noticed Lily frantically gesticulating at her. The penny dropped. She turned very red and burst into hopeless giggles.

"Caitlyn! *The* Caitlyn! Oh, wow, come in. It's so lovely to meet you!"

"I hope it's all right that I invited my sister to join us?" said Ms Bright.

Sam reached out and squeezed her arm. "Of course. This is a night made for family."

At the stroke of midnight, everyone spilled on to the beach, where Sam's papa started to light fireworks, ignoring the concerned yelps of his husband each time one went awry. An out-of-tune chorus of "Auld Lang Syne" broke out.

"So is this song written in couplets?" asked Jay.

"Don't," groaned Sam. "I've had enough couplets to last me a lifetime."

"What's it all about anyway? Why can't these old-timey poets just say what they mean?" said Lily.

Sam put an arm round each of them and squeezed

them tight. "It's about friends, you uncultured swine. It's about best friends."

Ms Bright was standing alone by the water's edge, watching the fireworks bloom in the sky, their reflections scattering across the sea.

"Happy New Year, Ms Bright."

"Happy New Year, Lily."

"Are you looking to see if your diamond has washed up? I've been keeping an eye out."

"My diamond?"

"The one I threw out of the lighthouse."

"Oh, Lily."

Ms Bright explained about seeing the diamond smash on the ground.

Lily frowned. "I didn't think a diamond would break like that."

"It wouldn't, sweetheart. It was a fake."

"I don't understand."

"I'm sorry, Lily. There probably never was a diamond. Just an old story, like I said."

"No, not that. I understand that. But why would a treasure hunt end in a fake diamond?"

"To show you that you'd come to the right place. Don't think like Snyde. A diamond isn't the only kind of treasure."

"So what was the treasure then? Do you know?"

"I know what I hope it was, yes."

"Why did the clues take us to the lighthouse?"

"So that it could do what all lighthouses do." She looked down at Lily, and Lily saw that her eyes were bright and shining with unspilled tears. "Guide someone safely home."

Thirty-Five

The sun rose on a hazy New Year's Day. Most of Edge slept soundly, some rolling over and swearing that they'd never go to such an outrageous party again. The town was filled with a freezing mist, throwing everything into soft focus, and the horizon between the sky and sea blurred and vanished. After the storm of the previous week, the air was fresh and cool, the breeze lifting Lily's hair, the tang of salt resting on her tongue. Shallow pools glimmered in the sand. Everything was washed in silver.

Lily, Sam and Jay had followed Ms Bright to the lighthouse. Caitlyn carried a bucket, passing it up to her sister. Water sloshed out on to her head and she squealed.

"Emily! Would you watch it?"

Sam, Jay and Lily exchanged delighted glances. They couldn't get used to seeing the sisters together. It was like seeing characters from a book step out into the real world. At the top, the wind whistled insistently through the broken window of the beacon room, making them all shiver.

They set to work, each grabbing a cloth and scrubbing at the years of dirt scumming the glass of the beacon room. Sam hoisted Lily on to her shoulders to reach the high parts. Piece by piece, the sea and the town in the distance came into view. Lily had guessed correctly. It was beautiful in the light. By mid-morning the glass was gleaming. Ms Bright stood back, one hand laced into her sister's, one raised to her eyes, peering out to sea, searching, searching.

The lighthouse had been built long before electricity was in regular use. The beacon was an enormous kerosene lantern, the light refracted through a complicated lens to produce the strong beam used to guide wandering ships. Ms Bright sent the three children back down to the lighthouse keeper's quarters while she and Caitlyn poured kerosene and lit the lamp. Lily looked around guiltily at the mess. She heaved the bookshelf back right-side up and picked up the scattered, mouldy books, arranging them neatly on the shelf. She walked over to the window and looked out at her town.

"Isn't it funny? Years ago, someone sat in exactly this spot looking out at exactly this view."

Sam grinned. "I remember when you used to say things like that as an insult. Now you sound almost ... impressed."

Lily stuck her tongue out. A yellow shard of light struck out suddenly across the water. Victorious yelps came from above them. Ms Bright stuck her head through the trapdoor.

"Come and see this."

They clambered up the ladder, eyes growing round at the sight of the colossal steady light burning at the centre of the tower. Ms Bright hunkered down, pointing to the enormous wheels underneath the lamp.

"Look, this is what makes the light turn."

She grasped the handle of one enormous wheel and pushed hard. For a few seconds it didn't move. Then, with an outraged creak, rust began to flake off and the wheel started to turn.

Lily looked at the lamp but it didn't move.

"Not yet. This doesn't turn the light, otherwise the lighthouse keeper would have had to stand up here all the time, turning the handle. You wind it up like a clock. Listen."

Lily cocked her head as Ms Bright continued to push the wheel. Something was stirring in the heart of the tower, groaning as though it had just been woken from a very long slumber. Sweat started to bead on Ms Bright's forehead but her eyes were shining excitedly.

"This handle pulls up a weight in the centre of the lighthouse. As the weight drops, it turns the cogs up here."

The wheel started to turn faster, gathering momentum, until with a dull clang it stopped. Ms Bright looked up at her sister, smiling, and took her hands from the handle. There was silence for a second and then a terrific rasping sound, as the ancient wheels battled the layers of rust encasing them. A series of cracks rang out and the cogs began to turn. The beam of light on the water started to move. The five of them cheered, jumping up and down. Lily peered closely at the enormous clockwork mechanism.

"How long does the weight take to drop?" asked Jay.

"I'm not sure," said Ms Bright. "Two or three hours, I think. Then we'll have to come back up and wind it again."

Sam whistled. "No wonder being a lighthouse keeper was a full-time job."

They climbed back down to the lighthouse keeper's quarters. Ms Bright stopped and looked around. Lily sidled up beside her.

"Are you thinking about your grandpa?"

Ms Bright nodded. "Hmm. It's funny to think that this was his home." She reached out a hand and stroked the back of the armchair. "I wonder if I could fix it up."

"To live in?" said Lily, looking around doubtfully.

Ms Bright laughed. "Do you think there's space for all of my books in here? No, not to live in. A space for the town, maybe. For people to come and visit. To see a piece of the past."

Lily smiled. "That sounds an awful lot like a museum."

"I suppose it does. Me and my museums."

"Without a museum, we never would have found you. Or the diamond. Or your treasure hunt."

Ms Bright put a hand to her mouth, as though thinking about the treasure hunt was too much for her to bear. Lily understood. Well, sort of. It was a hard thing to imagine.

They climbed down to the beach, craning their necks back to see the flame at the top of the lighthouse. Sam went to buy chips. They sat on the sea wall, licking salt from their fingers, rolling hot chips in their mouths. Lily tried not to fidget, tried to ignore the sick, rocking feeling in her stomach. They made forced conversation and then, after a while, fell into silence.

The sun skimmed along the top of the water, barely lighting the sky as the day drew on. The beam of the lighthouse stopped moving. Caitlyn sighed and started the long climb back to the beacon room. Ms Bright wandered along the sand, kicking at it with her toes.

"I can't bear this," said Sam.

"Imagine how they must be feeling," said Lily.

"She says that she's not even daring to hope," said Jay.

"Of course she is," said Lily. "You couldn't help but hope. It's what people do."

The sisters returned to the bench, their faces pale and pinched. The sun dipped lower in the sky. Ms Bright turned to the three, offering a shaky, watery smile.

"I'm not sure how long we should sit for."

Lily slid her cold hand into Ms Bright's. "She's coming, Ms Bright. She's coming."

Ms Bright smiled at Lily, but she couldn't help her eyes being pulled to the horizon. Searching, searching. Lily swallowed hard.

Suddenly Lily leapt to the top of the wall. She put her hand to her eyes, squinting out at the sea. A green speck was just visible in the mass of grey. She waved her arms, jumping up and down.

"There's a boat! There's a boat! I can see a boat!"

The others scrambled to their feet, desperately peering out towards the horizon.

"We're a seaside town, Lily. We get lots of boats," said Ms Bright, failing to hide the dry tremor in her voice. Her hands were shaking.

The green dot grew bigger, agonisingly slowly. Lily felt as though she might lose her mind. Ms Bright's knuckles were white, nails digging crimson crescents into her palms. Caitlyn's hand worried at her chest, beating an irregular pattern over her heart. Closer, ever closer the boat crept, illuminated periodically in the swinging beam of the lighthouse.

Ms Bright let out an almighty cry and started to run, hand in hand with Caitlyn, hair and coats streaming wildly behind them, feet throwing up enormous clods of sand. She almost lost her footing more than once, her heart moving faster than her feet could keep up with. The three children ran after them, legs pumping, arms thrown out in front to help keep their balance. They stopped on the edge of the sea, their boots slapping into the water. Ms Bright and her sister did not.

They ran, screaming as the water nipped at their feet, ploughing forward until it covered their ankles, their knees. Ms Bright's coat grew heavy as it filled with water, floating behind her like a magnificent jellyfish, tugging her back towards the shore. She shrugged it off, struggling to escape it as the water rose around her waist. Tears streamed down her face as the woman in the boat leapt into the water and ran towards them, water splashing wildly around. The sea slowed their pace, so that Lily seemed to see it all in slow motion.

At last the women reached each other, joining like drops of water, a tangle of indistinguishable arms and legs and screams as the two sisters threw themselves into their mother's arms. Joanie McCrae disentangled herself from her daughters, holding them at arm's length, cupping their faces in her hands. Their shoulders bounced with sobs and shivers. Caitlyn and Ms Bright clutched at their mother. Twenty years after first returning to Edge to find her house empty, her daughters gone, Joanie McCrae had found her way home.

Thirty-Six

They sat in Ms Bright's little kitchen, the three women sneaking shy glances at each other over cups of tea. Joanie was bundled into an enormous tartan blanket by Ms Bright and stared in obvious delight at this new, adult Emily. The windows were fogged with condensation from the soaking clothes on the radiators. Finally Lily couldn't take it any more. Grown-ups were useless.

"So what happened?"

"*Lily,*" said Ms Bright.

Joanie laughed. "No, no, it's OK." She ran a hand through her hair. "I've thought so many times about what I would say to both of you if I found you. But now that it's here, I don't know how to explain."

"It's OK, Mum," said Caitlyn, reaching for her hand.

Joanie lifted her cup to her lips but didn't drink. She set it back down and squeezed her eyes shut.

"Someone found me a few towns away the next morning. After … after he threw me from the boat. I was clinging to the rocks, half dead, totally delirious.

I couldn't even tell them my name. I was just yelling about my daughters and a diamond. It was weeks before I was well enough to travel. By the time I got back to Edge, you were gone. I was sure he'd taken you."

Her voice cracked. Ms Bright winced. Joanie was quiet for a long time but when she spoke again, her voice was stronger.

"I went to the police, of course. They took me seriously to start with, two missing kids. But I made the mistake of telling them what happened to me. Stupid. I sounded crazy. Diamonds and pirates, and evil men throwing people from boats. I'm not sure they even really believed I was Joanie McCrae. They sent me off with a pat on the head and an assurance that they'd do their best to find my daughters."

"They didn't believe us either," said Sam. "Threw us out and told us off for wasting police time."

"I got a bit lost after that. I'd go back to the old house and just sit in our rooms, staring at the walls. And then one day I remembered the loose board in Emily's room."

Ms Bright's head jerked up. Joanie smiled and closed her eyes, a tear escaping down her cheek.

"That was the happiest moment of my life. Second happiest now. Because when I saw your treasures hidden, Emily, I knew you were out there. I knew he hadn't got you. There was no trace of you, Caitlyn, but I always hoped. I always hoped that if I found Emily, I'd find you too. I hid in the house for weeks, hoping you'd come back. But I was losing my mind. Living in a shell of our old life, terrified that Snyde was going to come back and finish the job."

"You had to get out," said Ms Bright.

"I went back to the town where I'd washed up. The woman who'd pulled me out of the water seemed to understand that I was running from something terrible. She was happy to help me start a new life as a new person. When I felt safe, I started looking for you. I even hired a private investigator."

Caitlyn looked stricken. "A private investigator?"

"We ran," said Ms Bright. "We thought it was Snyde tracking us and we ran."

Joanie shook her head. "No way to tell, my loves.

I'm sure he had people looking for you too. After a while, I realised I wasn't going to find you. So I had to make sure that if you ever found your way home, you knew to look for me. I couldn't figure out how to make sure you could find me but Snyde couldn't. And then I thought of our games, Emily."

"The treasure hunts," said Ms Bright.

"Exactly. I needed a puzzle. A puzzle that didn't lead to me but that led to something that would tell you I was out there, that would tell you how to find me when it was safe."

"The diamond in the lantern," said Ms Bright.

"A treasure. Straight out of your bedtime stories."

Ms Bright nodded. "That was when I knew it had to be you. I thought of you before, when I found the museum. But it just didn't seem possible."

Joanie cupped Ms Bright's face in her hand. "Of course not. I created a puzzle for a curious, incorrigible little girl. I was never thinking of you as an adult. Silly."

Ms Bright smiled at Lily. "Luckily for all of us, your puzzle found exactly the right curious, incorrigible little girl." She pulled her mother into her arms.

Lily flushed and turned to look out of the window. The distant lighthouse beam swung, lighting up the town in ferocious colour for a second. She thought of the library and the museum. She thought of Ms Hanan's classroom and Sam's bedroom window. She thought of Sam's dad's lasagne and her mum's flattened rosebush and Costello snoozing in the garden. She thought of her mum shuffling around their kitchen, singing terribly. She thought of their kitchen table, and all of the adventures she would hatch there. She smiled. The McCraes weren't the only ones who had found their way home.

Acknowledgements

This book has passed through so many hands that to thank all of them would take a whole other book.

Thank you to my mum and dad for funding my early notebook habit, feeding my imagination and teaching me to be funny. Thank you to Kiera for being my consultant on young people things and to Sophie for being so horrifyingly carsick that I started telling stories to distract her. Thank you to the usual suspects, to Karla, Colin, Chris and Jenni, to my Auntie Kathleen, my Granny Rosie, my Grampa Dougie and my Grandad. Thank you to my beloved niblings, Ross and Hannah, who keep me from growing up. In every sense that matters, you made me.

Thank you to Johnstone Library, PACE Youth Theatre and everyone at Castlehead High School - especially Ms Liston, who realised early on that the wee quiet lassie had a voice.

Thank you to Ruth Mainland, Victoria Craig, Suzanne Hewings, Eddie Bowers and Rebecca Martinho for being relentlessly excited for me, even when I'm being ridiculous, which is often. You are the greatest and I love you. IDST. Thank you to Kathryn Foxfield, whose feedback changed the entire course of this book.

Thank you to the incredible Julia Silk, who was a friend and champion long before she became my agent. I couldn't have asked for a better person at my side on this journey.

Thank you to Tom Bonnick, who descended into my Twitter DMs like a deus ex machina and polished my words until they sparkled. Thank you for not only accepting but delighting in the book's (and the author's) oddities and for ... well, for making a dream come true. Thank you to everyone at Nosy Crow for transforming my funny little story into the gorgeous object you now hold in your hands.

Thank you most of all to Niall, for filling my life with adventures big and small, for bottomless cups of tea, for thinking I'm the best person in the world despite all evidence to the contrary and for always, always believing I could do this. This book could not have been written without you.